WHITEWATER CROSSING

To Dewey,
Merry Christmas. (2009)

Roy Bush

11/21/09

CLEO
(CATSALA)

WHITEWATER CROSSING

A Casey Jones
Columbia River
Adventure

Roy W. Bush

ELDERBERRY PRESS, INC.

Illustrated by Raven OKeefe
Cover art is Raven O'Keefe's depiction of Native Americans fishing at Celilo Falls before it was inundated by The Dalles Dam on March 10, 1957.

Elderberry Press, Inc.
1393 Old Homestead Drive, Second Floor
Oakland, Oregon 97462–9506.
E MAIL: editor@elderberrypress.com
TEL/FAX: 541. 459. 6043
www. elderberrypress.com

Available from your favorite bookstore, amazon.com, or from our 24- hour order line: 1. 800. 431. 1579

Library of Congress Control Number: 2009933144
Publisher's Catalog—in—Publication Data
Whitewater Crossing / Roy W. Bush
ISBN 10:   1-934956-19-8
ISBN 13: 978-1-934956-19-9

1. Young Adult - Fiction
2. Adventure - Fiction
3. Horses - Fiction
4. Wild Animals - Fiction
5. Coming of Age - Fiction
6. Northwest history

This book was written, printed and bound in the United States of America.

My thanks to Jerome Buckmier for reading the first Casey Jones Adventure, Cry Of The Goshawk, to his students, and for his encouragement during the writing of this sequel.

To the students and staff of The School for the Blind, Vancouver, Washington.

one

ON THE TRAIL

I rode out in the dark of early morning leaving the K2 Ranch behind, looked up and thrilled to the bright November constellations. With Signus the Swan overhead, and Polaris over my shoulder I headed across the Serpentine at the wood bridge and up the bluff. Within minutes, my fine cowpony, Jasper, and I began to cross a wide expanse of lush grass that famously came up to a horse's belly.

I leaned down and patted Jasper on the neck. "Hey fella, with grass like this, I can see why they call this area the Horse Heaven Hills."

As we loped along I thought, "How strange life can be. Here I am, Casey Jones, a New York City kid who has landed way out here in the state of Washington to live on the legendary K2 Ranch."

On this beautiful morning with winter on the way, my head filled with images thick as snowflakes . . . thoughts of the old neighborhood swirled in my head, football at school, the fights and the friendships.

There was the small apartment in Brooklyn where Mom, Dad and I had lived our happy lives together. I'd never asked them if they'd named me after the famous railroad engineer who'd died trying to avoid a train wreck, but when asked about being related to him, I just answer, "No, Jones is a common name."

Jasper seemed to love being out here. His smooth gait allowed me to revive memories of the fine folks who lived in our tenement house, especially the kindly Mr. Lambrusco, who taught me to love history and music. But mostly I remembered my loving Dad. Back then he worked long, hard hours but still had time for me. Boy! Did I ever love those Saturday afternoons as we washed down hot dogs with big cups of frothy cola and cheered on our winning team, the Brooklyn Dodgers.

Now in the year 1921, I don't often look back to when Dad died on the job following an operation, and the difficult days that followed. I had to leave Mom and head west to live with relatives, so scared I felt like jumping off the train and running back.

I'd ridden the train through Chicago, across the plains, over the Rocky Mountains, and down again into the fertile valley drained by the Serpentine where I'd been warmly welcomed by my new family.

My life in Brooklyn had its good points, but out here . . . well, there's adventure! That began when I met Kinsman family . . . my three lively girl cousins and their parents. I got swept up in their lifestyle. At first I was bowled over by their huge manor house in Arborville. Then, I was so amazed by their huge K2 Ranch I fell into an irrigation ditch my first day there.

Now Mom has followed me here and I think this new life in central Washington is everything Dad would have wanted for us.

I'm 17 and feel like a real cowhand. I'm being trained by my Uncle Harry to take on more responsibility. Like right now he's sending me to see a man down in Oregon. I have instructions to buy twenty bales of wool and get them shipped by barge down the Columbia River to a customer of ours in Portland.

Last night rain had soaked these broad Horse Heaven Hills and I breathed deeply, loving the odor of damp grass and moist earth. On this part of the journey, Jasper's smooth canter continued for over two hours before he slowed up to a nervous trot.

"Hey! What is it, fella? Do you sense something I don't?"

Then I heard the eerie thunder of many hooves. Jasper moved from side to side and bobbed his head.

"Whoa Jasper! Whoa boy!" I patted Jasper's neck to soothe him and tingled all over as I realized that a herd of wild horses was crossing the trail just ahead.

"Skidoo! Sure wish I could see those beautiful animals . . . running wild and free. Maybe on the return trip in full daylight we will."

Reaching a highpoint overlooking the gorge that separates Washington and Oregon, Mt. Hood appeared in the distance . . . its peak, like a carnival small Snow cone, glistened pale rose in the rays of the rising sun.

I caught my breath as the mighty Columbia River appeared below, a shimmering silver ribbon, wide and full, flowing west to a waiting Pacific Ocean. The vapor of my breath rose in the chill air and I paused to savor the extraordinary view before urging Jasper to a cautious, hour-long trot down to the riverbank where we faced a ferry ride to the Oregon side. A bit farther on we would meet the man who raised sheep.

My ranch hand friend, Cal Paluskin, had told me about the crossing of this river named for Columbus. "You and the horse will be standing on the water while seagulls fly overhead," he'd said.

Though forewarned, when I saw how we were to cross, I was amazed. Midway on the broad span of water, a small steam-powered tugboat labored, urging a barge toward a dock just below us.

The makeshift ferry arrived just as Jasper and I came to the dock. I smelled the smoke from the tugboat as the red-faced ferryman in overalls waited for a wagon and team of horses to clatter off the barge and onto the dock. Then he called out to me with an outstretched hand, black with coal dust. "That'll be five cents for you and a nickel for the horse."

As we trotted onto the barge, Jasper rolled his eyes and clomped his hooves on the deck . . . the clip clop reverberating in the hollowness below.

"Easy there, boy. There's a lot of water down there, but you and I are going to stay dry as a clump of sagebrush."

We were the only passengers, so the ferryman cast off the mooring line. He stepped into the pilothouse, spun the wheel, and threw the tug into reverse before shifting into full speed ahead. The barge, tethered to the tug by heavy hawsers, glided into the swirling waters with a shudder.

After ten minutes of chuffing and churning up a foamy wake, the ferry docked on the Oregon side.

Jasper seemed pleased to be on solid footing once more. He pranced around and tossed his fine head. When I spurred him on, he leaped ahead, pleased to be back on solid ground.

We rode east for several minutes scanning the riverbank for the man who raised sheep.

Then, while still two hundred yards distant, I caught sight of him. We exchanged a high-sign of friendship and greeted each other with a smile.

"Have you come up from the Umatilla?" I asked.

"Umm, I have . . . and you from Arborville?"

I nodded yes. A Native American in his thirties, he wore a beautiful blue and red woolen jacket, a deerskin vest and riding pants. His long raven hair framed a handsome face. He smiled with his eyes as I continued.

"I'm Casey Jones from the K2 ranch. My uncle, Harry Kinsman, sent me."

"I am Rightfoot." He turned, pointing at the river's edge. "Just there you can see the bales on the dock where my brothers left them. If you come to buy the wool from the spring shearing, we can load them on the barge just below."

I glanced around, looking for a place to make camp.

Rightfoot with the same idea in mind said, "over there," nodding toward a rocky outcrop, "under the overhang we'll have shelter from the wind."

"Yes, we can fix a meal and do the deal." I noted a scattering of wood for a fire.

Despite damp wood, Rightfoot quickly got a fire going and I placed my small, galvanized coffeepot filled with water by it, then pulled out the cash for the wool purchase. I counted out the amount Uncle Harry had agreed to and handed it over. Rightfoot accepted the greenbacks with a nod. I handed him my pen and smoothed out a Bill of Sale on my saddlebag. He quickly signed on the proper line.

On the loading dock we transferred the large bales of wool to the barge and returned to the fire.

In minutes we prepared a tasty meal of boiled venison and wild onions, seasoned with sage; frybread and cooked greens picked from the roadside.

I remembered it was Thanksgiving Day. With an appetite sharpened by fresh air and time on the trail, I enjoyed the simple meal as we topped it off with several molasses cookies from K2's kitchen.

As we leaned back and sipped our coffee, I felt happiness and peace . . . so thankful for this life that I had come to live far from my eastern origins. With a sigh of contentment I gazed out across the shimmering water to the beautiful hillside beyond.

"How far to the ocean?" I asked.

"I have traveled there only once . . . as a boy with my father."

Rightfoot gazed downstream and frowned, seeming to recall a difficult journey. "I think it took us ten days by horse." Then he smiled. "But we stopped a day or so to fish for salmon at Celilo."

I'd heard of Celilo, the waterfall that interrupted the mighty river's flow from one bank to the other and roiled the waters below. Exciting tales of thousands of salmon swimming upstream and jumping the falls during the spawning season had made me curious, but I thought better of pursuing details of native fishing. Instead, I asked, "Will you and your people have more wool to sell?"

Rightfoot stared at the fire for several seconds.

"I think yes." Then after another pause he continued. "Some of the older ones don't like us raising sheep. They want the old ways . . . before we began to raise them."

"How do you feel about it?" I asked.

"I like the sheep . . . watching the dogs work the band. They know every move, even before a sheep makes it. And I like caring for the lambs in the spring."

He paused and went on. "The older ones know that we need the money from wool, sheepskins and meat, but they won't say it."

After the last swallow of coffee, Rightfoot put down his cup. Shading his eyes with his hand, he squinted upstream. "I think our boat comes," he observed. "Soon the wool will float down to Portland."

"Yes, the tugboat will guide the barge downstream, all the way to the warehouse of the Johnsen Company. They will make it into fine blankets, and sweaters and jackets, like the one you're wearing."

Rightfoot carefully tightened the drawstrings on the deer-skin money pouch slung around his neck. A man of few words, he nodded farewell and mounted his appaloosa. I watched horse and rider move up the bluff toward the high rim of the gorge. I imagined him setting his horse to a canter as he made his way back to the village on the banks of the Umatilla.

On the far side he might cross a branch of the old Oregon Trail, the route that had been traversed by uncounted thousands of pioneers moving west.

No more daydreaming now. I swung into the saddle for the return trip to K2. The business part of this trip now behind us, Jasper smoothly set a lively pace, quickening to the old Lewis and Clark Trail.

But just then, as we sped downstream, I noticed a hunched-over rider on a large dark horse swiftly moving down the hill to the ferry landing on the other side.

I wondered, "What kind of person would ride all bent over like that, wearing a black hat and long leather cape?"

Despite the warming rays of the mid-day sun, something about the mysterious horseman gave me a chill.

Eager to divert my mind away from the sinister figure, I thought of Lewis and Clark.

I felt a tingle of excitement as we traveled the route of the Corps of Discovery, commissioned by President Jefferson to explore the Louisiana Purchase.

Mr. Lambrusco had loaned me a book that showed the route they'd taken. In 1802 they'd made their way from St. Louis, through the wilderness of what is now Missouri, North Dakota, Montana, Idaho, Washington and Oregon to the Pacific Ocean.

For hours at a time, I'd pored over the photos of the actual maps, sketches of plants and Merriweather Lewis's many drawings of animals and birds they'd seen.

Included were exact descriptions of the Native Americans they'd met along the way. At the time I read about all of this, I hadn't had any idea that I'd actually come to be here, traveling the early explorers' route on the Columbia.

I looked out at the river and I wondered just how I would go about making a boat from trees along the shore as they had done. I'd read that they had to carry their boats overland around Celilo Falls on their way to the Pacific. What sturdy men they must have been! And how determined they were to successfully complete their mission.

two

AMBUSHED

I prided myself for doing a man's job and my heart sang with satisfaction. Buying the wool for shipment had been easy. Now I looked forward to the journey home.

Jasper and I were making good time, but with the sun showing mid-afternoon, I knew we would be spending the night in the open . . . somewhere back up and beyond the river. No problem, I was prepared. I had a bedroll and food for another warm meal.

I smiled at the clouds forming up in the west, pleased that I'd packed my oilskin poncho. Camping out overnight would be part of the overall adventure.

I thought of the dark rider I'd seen after the meeting with Rightfoot. We'd not met on the trail, so I assumed that this traveler had journeyed downstream after taking the ferry.

Suddenly, as we came around a twist in the trail, a large rock tumbled down and bounced in front of us. It didn't block the trail, but Jasper reared and I calmed him as best I could.

"Whoa Jasper! Settle down boy. We need to check this out."

At that moment a dark figure loomed on my left, fiercely

ramming my shoulder with a rifle butt, knocking me off Jasper.

My right arm hit first and I felt a bone snap an instant before my head slammed back.

My attacker took two giant strides, mounted Jasper, brought him around, and spurred him to a full gallop.

Jasper might have resisted the rider if I'd been able to shout to him, but when I struggled to call him back, no breath would come.

I managed to turn my head a bit. "Jasper! JASPER!" I croaked. In total agony, I watched horse and rider gallop up a slight rise and then disappear from sight down the far side, heading upstream.

What misery! Straining to get my breath, the searing pain in my arm was more than I could bear.

I fell back, gasping as a chill breeze picked up. On bare ground, stabs of cold began to penetrate my coat as the awful truth sank in. I'D LOST JASPER, MY WONDERFUL HORSE! STOLEN!

Once back in Brooklyn, while getting up on a pair of homemade stilts, I'd fallen backward and had the breath knocked out of me. Now I re-lived those agonizing moments when I thought I would never breathe again. But at last, my racking gasps stopped as air returned to my deflated lungs.

Last year I'd been injured to the point of death, and that incident had also involved a horse. Now, again in mortal danger, I lay helpless, unable to move. Several times I almost blacked out from the pain in my arm, but was revived by an icy wind in my face.

After what must have been hours I struggled to sit up. I managed to slide over and lean against a log. I found my broad-brimmed western hat within reach. Now I could keep my throbbing head warm and look around. Shivering and miserable, I took stock of my injuries. I knew my arm was broken, but I wasn't bleeding anywhere.

I couldn't predict when I'd be able to walk, and I prayed, "Lord, help me to survive and get Jasper back."

Shivering now, it helped my spirits some to note that the windstorm was passing by with only a few drops of rain. And then I heard a small whinny, a nickering from behind me.

My heart sang, "Jasper! You've come back to me! Of course you would . . . just as soon as you got the chance."

How I would love to hug him, smell his horseiness, ride out with him again. But before I could turn to greet him, I slipped into darkness.

I came to, still sitting by the log with a brutally stiff neck and searing pain in arm and head. The last rays of the sun glared off the river. Then, I remembered all that had happened, I thought that Jasper had returned to me. Yes! I would endure anything, now that my horse was back with me! Together, we'd get home somehow.

I twisted my neck and gazed around, eagerly looking for Jasper, and there, off to one side, a horse was peacefully cropping grass. I sobbed as I looked more closely. Instead of my youthful, well-groomed roan, my bleary eyes focused on a scraggly old horse, whose unkempt dark brown flanks were caked with mud. I thought that my feverish mind was playing tricks on me. I closed my eyes to shut out the awful sight and again, darkness took over.

A terrifying rumbling roused me in the black of night. My first thought was of thunder. But the fearful sound went on and on as the ground shook beneath me. My tortured mind imagined a cattle stampede. Then the rumble suddenly stopped.

The moon gleamed down from a clear sky. It seemed a bad omen because now I burned with a fever and felt near death.

In a delirious state, I dreamt that Jasper and I were back

on the barge about to go over a waterfall. I saw Jasper pawing the deck, and heard his wild neighing, pleading for me to save him. I awoke with a start and a shiver.

My arm seemed on fire and my throat burned with thirst, but I welcomed the warmth of the morning sun. Amid all of this I wondered about Jasper. Had his return been a dream . . . the scruffy horse a nightmare?

I eagerly looked around but saw no horse. I made an effort to get up, steeling myself against the pain I sat on the log. Then minutes later, I again I heard something behind me and turned to find the brown horse looking at me with sorrowful eyes. He looked as miserable as I felt.

What was happening?

Then it came to me. "Of course! The one who stole Jasper had left this old nag behind."

I had to face reality. "Survive! Then go after the horse thief!"

With new resolve I thought, "Does this old horse have a saddle?"

I painfully turned to look over my shoulder. "Yes! And a canteen too!"

I struggled to my knees as the horse drew near enough for me to grab a stirrup, pull myself up and grab the canteen. Unconcerned about who might have been drinking from it, I took several swallows. The water was brackish and bad tasting . . . no matter. It soothed my fevered throat.

Then I shouted, "Skidoo!" as I discovered a heavy woolen blanket tied behind the saddle. It was warm from the close contact with the horse. I sank down and wrapped it around my shivering shoulders. With protection from the cold, I dozed off.

three

A PASSERBY

*T*he brilliant sun raised my spirits. No longer shivering, I had a sense of drifting on a cloud. I gazed up to a blue sky and realized that I might be leaving this painful world. Was there no hope? I prayed for help.

Oh, this journey to Oregon had begun so well. I loved being on the trail. I'd felt so grown-up, transacting K2 business. It was my first chance to show Uncle Harry that I could travel out and close a deal on my own.

When we'd talked about it, he'd suggested that one of the ranch hands come along with me. But I'd protested so he agreed to my going it alone.

So here I am, too weak to walk or mount a horse, with no food. I realized I'd need help to make it. And just then, I looked up to see help on the way.

A large man dressed in an Alaskan-type parka and heavy boots tramped his way up the trail. I joyfully raised my hand. "Hello!"

He shouted, "Hello! Do you need some help?"

"Yes! Yes I do."

The man heard my story as he tended my broken right

arm. Ripping his bandana into strips, he fashioned a splint from a piece of wood found nearby. When he pulled on my arm to bring the broken ends of bone together, I screamed with pain.

He helped me on with my shirt and noticed my left shoulder.

"You have a nasty bruise there."

"I got that when the outlaw knocked me off my horse with his rifle butt."

With my head swimming, he helped me onto the old horse and led me up the embankment to a set of railroad tracks. The railroad! Of course! That accounted for the rumbling in the night.

As we traveled, I gratefully chewed on a hunk of beef jerky from his pack and counted my blessings as he spoke.

"I floated by you in my keelboat a few minutes ago. I'm on a geology trip . . . caught sight of you just below that interesting rock outcrop up above. You looked in a bad way so I put in to shore."

He stopped to pat the nag on the neck. "Looks like the horse here is strong enough. He was down getting a drink out of the river when I came up, and he's had grass to eat. The dry grass this time of year is full of nourishment, almost like alfalfa hay. He appears to have been ridden hard . . . probably needed a rest."

I thought, "Where is this fella taking me?" Then my heart jumped as I saw an outfit car, used by railroad crews who maintained the roadbed and tracks. There would be bunks and a stove in it . . . maybe even some canned goods.

We came alongside. I saw bars over the windows and with a thrill of excitement noticed that the heavy door was secured by a familiar railroad padlock. I thought, "I'll bet my railroad key will fit that lock!"

Because Uncle Harry is a Northern Pacific Railroad Superintendent, he had been giving me some experience in the Arborville depot. He'd issued me what's known as a switch key. All of the hand-operated rail switches are locked with a similar padlock and the keys for them are standard.

My kind helper examined the lock. "Hmm. Too heavy to break . . . I'll have to try some other way to get in. We need to get inside, build a fire and get a hot meal in you."

I pulled out my key and said, "Try this."

The lock popped open and the man handed the key back to me. "That's really astonishing! After we get you fixed up, you must tell me where you got hold of a railroad master key."

Inside, I stretched out on a bunk and my rescuer busied himself with the stove.

"I'm Lear Bennett, a University of Washington geology professor. I intend to write a report on this section of the river."

"I'm Casey Jones," I replied. "I'm from Arborville by way of Brooklyn, New York."

"Casey Jones, eh. Despite your railroad connection, I'll bet you are no relation to the famous Casey Jones, the engineer who died trying to avoid a train wreck."

"No, Jones is a common name." I said, giving my usual response.

"Well, now that the wood stove has a roaring fire in it, I'll take your horse, ride to my boat and bring back a can of stew and some sourdough biscuits."

I heard Lear Bennett gallop off and I thought, "Well, that old horse is better than no horse at all. Thanks to him, we'll soon have a hot meal."

Then, snug in my blanket, I made a mental note to think of a name for him. While thinking of names, I realized that the geologist's name was familiar to me. I had met Lear Bennett before! Later, while wolfing down a plate of delicious stew and biscuits, I remembered where.

"Dr. Bennett, last year, another uncle of mine, Carl Coleman, and I met you on the steamboat Sitka Seafarer.

"You know, Casey, I felt that we'd met before. Yes, we were on our way back to Seattle from Ketchikan."

"Right. You told us of the huge United States Territory of Alaska and many interesting facts . . . especially about its size and the abundance of natural resources up there."

"I remember our onboard conversation now. I think I also encouraged you to consider making that land of opportunity part of your future."

"Yes, Lear. I've thought of checking out Alaska with a possibility of settling up there. But I'm still in high school and it appears I have a future in Arborville . . . running a large ranch some day, working on the railroad, or both."

Lear Bennett smiled. "Hmm, I see. Apparently you are well connected there."

After our simple meal, Lear Bennett produced a bottle of liniment. "Casey, would you like me to rub some of this on your bruised shoulder?"

"Skidoo! I sure would." I replied.

Lear gently applied the liniment and it helped take away some of the soreness.

For the next hour, Lear Bennett and I talked of many things. I described how I'd been ambushed and he described his adventures on the upper Columbia.

"Casey, the Columbia is the Northwest's longest river. It flows 1243 miles from its source, Lake Columbia in Canada to its mouth at Astoria where it is six miles wide. It is the largest West Coast river to empty into the Pacific."

"I've lived out west for over a year, but had no idea the Columbia was so grand a waterway." I said sincerely.

Lear Bennett smiled as he went on. "This gorge we're in

is amazing too. Geologically, it's one of the most interesting anywhere. Over its 400 mile length, the river drops 4500 feet. As the Columbia cut its way through, it formed many sheer cliffs and 77 waterfalls spill from them."

I reflected a minute on Dr. Bennett's astonishing description, then asked, "Lear, do you ever take your students on field trips to this area?"

"I do . . . mostly those students who are in advanced study. But the trip I'm on now is filling the gaps in my knowledge of this part of the river. You see, I'm writing a textbook about the Columbia and its tributaries, the 260,000 square mile watershed."

"Skidoo!" Would I ever like to go along on one of your field trips . . . and get a copy of your book when its done, too."

"Well, Casey, from what I know about you, I think you would be an asset to any outdoor study group. I'd be pleased to have you sign up for a field trip . . . as soon as you graduate from high school, that is. And as for acquiring a copy of my text, well, I'll arrange to send you an autographed copy just as soon as it's published."

"Well! That's generous of you, Lear. Thanks in advance."

Then I added, "Lear, I appreciate all you have done for me, you saved my life. But I'm going to make it O.K. now. I shouldn't keep you from your work any longer."

He looked skeptical. So I went on. "My fever seems to be gone and I'm quickly getting my strength back. I know I'll be able to ride again by tomorrow morning. Then, too, my family in Arborville will be worried. I need to let them know that I'm O.K. so they won't search for me. My uncle mentioned train station just downstream at The Dalles. If you're heading there, maybe you could send a telegram to my uncle, Harry Kinsman. You could just address it to the train depot in Arborville, where he works."

"All right, Casey, I'll do as you say, but I insist on staying the night first. Then, if you're enough improved, I'll be on my way after breakfast. And yes, I'll be pleased to send that telegram."

four

TRACKING JASPER

*L*ear was as good as his word. Soon after sunup, he stoked up the fire and set out another can of stew for me. After a breakfast of bacon, sourdough biscuits and coffee, he'd saddled the horse and asked, "Are you certain you'll be able to mount up?"

I stood up and raised my left arm. "Yes. See, thanks to you, I'm on the mend."

The morning had begun with a cloudless sky and the promise of a warmer day. Impelled by thoughts of tracking down the horse thief, I rousted myself two minutes after Lear left. I let the fire burn down and rolled the can of stew and the liniment in the blanket and tied it on in back of the saddle.

I snapped the padlock on the door, and turned to look at my replacement horse. He needed care that I couldn't give him. I thought of brushing the mud off his flanks, but with my right arm in a sling and my left shoulder still sore, I couldn't even do that simple chore.

It was time to move on. Unlike Jasper, when the first time I'd mounted him he had moved just wrong and I'd fallen in the dust, this horse stood still as I struggled to rise up in the stirrup and swing my leg over. Whatever his shortcomings, this horse was steady as a rock for me. We moved smoothly back down to the trail and headed upstream again, to where I'd caught my last glimpse of Jasper.

The horse thief had an eighteen hour head start, but now as I began to track him, I had one thing in my favor. Last month Jasper had thrown the shoe from his right rear hoof. Mr. Tyson, the K2 blacksmith and I had replaced it. I recalled that the new shoe had three diamond marks on it. Now, as we ambled along, doubling back on yesterday's route, I carefully scanned the earth below.

At first I couldn't distinguish Jasper's diamond-marked horseshoe print from all the others, but then I spotted it! And a few feet further on, another and another. I'd picked up Jasper's trail and that of the horse thief as surely as if he'd splashed a yellow paint mark every ten feet.

We were making good time now. Impressed with this big animal, I decided he needed to have a name.

"Say Horse," I said. "We're doubling back on the trail. I think I have a name for you. Hmm . . . doublin' back. Yes, I dub you Dublin."

Maybe Dublin liked his new name and my talking to him. He seemed to be making a conscious effort to make my ride smooth, and I flowed with his rhythm. I loved him for that. My injuries couldn't take any rough bouncing around.

On upstream we came to a fork in the trail. Still following the telltale hoof print, we quickly took the branch that veered off to the southeast.

Just then we came up to a man on horseback. The rider, in a dusty uniform of sorts, jumped off as we approached. A colorful deputy sheriff's patch flashed from his broad-brimmed hat and blue jacket.

I slowed down. "Whoa, Dublin."

On his hip was slung a holster, and with eyes blazing, he suddenly drew his pistol.

"Rein up there!" he shouted while running toward us. "Get yer hands up!"

Sore arm forgotten, I did the best I could to comply.

"Get down offun that horse," he yelled.

"Yes sir . . . right away," I replied as I threw my leg over and slipped to the ground.

"Down on yer knees," he barked as he looked me over.

"Where's yer gun? And where's the stuff ya stole from that settler ya bushwhacked?" he asked as he patted the saddlebag.

"I was ambushed," I cried frantically. "I don't have anything!"

Even with my arm in a sling, I was roughly handcuffed, hands in front, then raised to my feet.

"Yeah, an' I spose ya gonna tell me that this hain't your hoss neither."

"Whoever attacked me, switched horses with me."

The deputy holstered his gun. Still not completely convinced, he asked, "What's yer name and where you from?"

"I'm Casey Jones from the K2 ranch near Arborville." I replied.

"Hmm, just what are you doin' down here on this trail?"

"Tracking the man who stole my horse."

The deputy spit sideways with a sneer. "Pshaw! Trackin'? How you doin' that?" he said scornfully. "I spose you get down on all fours and sniff the hoof prints like an ol' hound dog."

"No! My horse's right rear shoe leaves a mark with three diamonds . . . like that one right there by your left foot." I said boldly.

The deputy looked down with a furrowed brow, saw the hoof mark, but remained unconvinced.

"How do I know you didn't jus' make that up?"

"Because I was heading home from buying a shipment of wool. If you'll take off these handcuffs, I'll show you the Bill of Sale."

"The cuffs stay on." The deputy said still frowning. "Tell me where the Bill of Sale is."

It was time for me to show some initiative. "I will. But first you tell me who you are and what you're doing on the trail."

The deputy blinked, then said, "I'm T. J. Torgeson, Deputy Sheriff of Benton County, on the trail of a cowardly outlaw who came close to killin' an old settler an' his wife . . . stole their hard earned stash. He was last seen heading up the gorge on a hoss like the one you came on."

I had to think fast. "So was it the ferryman who told you that? Maybe he also told you the man on this horse was wearing a dark hat and a long leather cape. I saw a rider like that too, down on the Washington side just after I came across."

"Well, Jones, you jus' talked yerself out of this one," said the deputy.

"Pshaw, when ya rode up, I shoulda set my sights more on you, 'steda this hoss."

Deputy Torgeson freed my hands and gave me a nod of apology. "Coulda seen right off you're not the man I'm after . . . woulda too, 'cept this big hoss caught my eye first."

"Well, the man you're after has my horse; a four year old. He's a roan with a white blaze and four stockings." I said, painfully rotating my stiff shoulder.

"White stockin' roan." He repeated.

With a twitch of his bushy moustache, and a "let's git after 'im!" the deputy leaped on his palomino and galloped off down the road. A nearby sign pointed southeast. The big black letters read: GREAT SALT LAKE -- 500 MI.

I rushed over to Dublin and soon we were in pursuit of the man I now thought of as TJ.

five

OREGON ODESSY

I pushed Dublin to the limit. TJ's strong palomino seemed tireless. Hour after hour we rode through the rolling brush-covered dry land with small, scattered, farm buildings and few signs of life.

As we sped across this arid land, I noticed TJ looking back at me from time to time. He seemed to know the country, because he suddenly took an unmarked trail and dropped down out of sight.

"Dublin, good thing you're fast enough to keep up or we'd not have seen TJ take this offshoot." I said, as I patted his neck.

A minute later, we came to a small, spring-fed stream running through a thicket of cottonwood trees. We found TJ bent over, filling his canteen. Without comment, I rode over, tethered Dublin, and refilled my canteen as well.

Then I noticed Dublin, so thirsty his dry mouth was foaming, waiting patiently. When I slipped his reins, he gave me a kindly look and stoically moved to drink from the stream alongside the palomino.

TJ rose up and pulled out a piece of hardtack biscuit that

he washed down with a few swigs of water. He offered me nothing, not even a word of encouragement. Then without so much as a glance in my direction, he stuffed a piece of jerky in his mouth and mounted up. Dublin and I followed, threading our way back up the dusty way to the road. I was glad for the steady pace. Down deep I wanted to keep going after the black-hearted villain who was up ahead somewhere riding my wonderful horse.

If the previous stretch had been hard and without letup, the next lap was a grueling marathon that pushed both horses to the limit. As the drier land gave way to cultivated farms with interspersed fields of corn shocks, the same pattern developed. We'd ride hard for miles, TJ would find roadside water, we'd rest momentarily and then once again be off at top speed.

TJ continued to look back every few minutes. Of course he was pursuing an outlaw who had a head start, but still, I got the idea that he was actually trying to leave Dublin and me behind.

Then, late in the afternoon, I thought he might lose us. I didn't know Dublin. I'd heard of horses being ridden until they dropped dead under their rider. If that happened at full speed, I'd go flying and probably wind up with a broken neck.

I eased up. This pace was a killer. Though my heart still ached for Jasper, for Dublin's sake, I had to stop soon.

As the sun set in a cloudbank I lost sight of the palomino. Then, as we came to a rise in the road, barely visible up ahead, I saw TJ bent over, peering at the roadway. I looked for Jasper's hoof mark but couldn't see one. That was it! It was too dark to see the diamond markings in the road. We had to make camp 'til sunup. With no bedroll or food, how would I to do that?

But TJ, the tireless tracker, had no intention of spending the chill night in the open. When Dublin and I came up to the spot where I'd last seen them, both horse and rider were gone.

I stood high in the saddle and noticed a barn and farmhouse looming in the haze of dusk and the pleasant smell of wood smoke drifted over to me.

In this cool fall evening, dank mist was rising from fallow farmland on either side of a narrow driveway. Up ahead I glimpsed TJ walking his horse, entering the paddock beyond the barn. I caught up to them just as a man in overalls and a floppy hat hailed us.

"Halloo there," he called out. "Looks like you two are lawmen." He paused staring at the steam coming from our winded horses. "You looking for a place to put up for the night?"

TJ stepped forward and extended his hand with a slight smile.

"Thank you sir for the offer. Indeed, I am in need of your hospitality."

Then with a raised eyebrow, he continued. "I am sheriff Torgeson of Benton County, up Washington way. I'm hot on the trail of a dangerous bushwhacker."

I noted that TJ was spreading it a bit thick for the benefit of the farmer while ignoring me.

As TJ began to walk his horse to cool him down after the hard ride, I slid off and also shook hands. "I'm Casey Jones. The outlaw we're tracking stole my horse."

"How dee do. I'm Jeb Connor. I'll show you fodder fer your horses in the barn and there's a place to bed down for the night there too. Over yonder's the pump and trough fer waterin' and washin' up. We were just fixin' to sit down to supper. You're just in time."

The kindly farmer led the way into the barn and turned to leave. "Come on in when you're ready and meet the missus."

I didn't want to ask TJ for help so I quickly stepped forward.

"Excuse me, sir." I began. "This is the horse the thief left me. He needs to be cared for. If there's someone who could get his saddle off and towel him down, I'm willing to pay a livery fee."

Mr. Connor looked at my broken arm. "Well, say, young man. Did you get that bad arm from the horse thief?"

"Yes, when he knocked me off my horse . . . didn't see him coming."

Mr. Connor turned to go. "I'll get Lou to come help you."

TJ led his horse to water, walked him to cool off more, then, back in the barn, hung the palomino's saddle, blanket and bridle on a rail. He got a cloth from his saddlebag and toweled him down, then led him to feed.

Still steaming, Dublin got his drink at the trough as I took a swallow from my canteen. Just then, the one I assumed was Lou, came out of the back door of the farmhouse wearing a sheepskin jacket, cowboy hat and jeans.

I put out my hand and Lou took it for a quick shake. A bit surprised, I blinked. Lou was a girl roughly my age.

"I'll help you with your horse," she said, taking the reins. "What's his name?"

"I've named him Dublin. But he's not my horse."

"My name is Louella, Lou for short."

"Hello, I'm Casey."

Louella was obviously a strong, no-nonsense farm girl. She had Dublin's saddle and blanket off in seconds. Then I heard her gasp. "Good God in Heaven!" she exclaimed turning to me with a look that could kill.

"What kind of miserable saddle tramp are you! Mistreating a good horse like this!" Louella, eyes blazing, stepped up to me and swung hard, aiming at my chin.

Somewhat saddle sore, I was a little slow to move away from the punch. I got a glancing blow on the jaw that knocked me over. This time I landed as a cowpoke does, with a side roll, careful to favor my broken arm, but still giving the pesky sore shoulder a painful bump.

How to explain? I looked up at poor Dublin's back . . . raw from too long under the saddle and I felt a pang of guilt. Obsessed with chasing after Jasper, I'd badly neglected Dublin. I deserved the rap on the chin. I pulled myself up and turned to Lou.

"He needs to be walked, cooled off, and dressed down with a medicated sponging."

Standing with clenched fists, she looked like she might swing at me again. Instead, she screamed, "PAW! HEY PAW! COME OUT HERE AND SEE THIS!"

Mr. Connor came running, rifle in hand, then stood looking at poor Dublin, steam rising from him . . . covered with sores and raw spots where the outlaw had raked him with his spurs.

Louella glowered at me, "You no account polecat! Not even a bushwhacker would mistreat a horse like that!"

I closed my eyes, and turned away. I had to fight back tears . . . my heart was close to breaking for Dublin who just stood there waiting for someone to help him.

Sometimes really bad things happen and there's no sense in trying to explain. I felt my excuses would ring hollow . . . make things even worse.

Then I got support from where I least expected it.

TJ stepped up. "Now Jones here hain't so guilty as he looks. At least a day before Jones got 'im, this horse was abused by the bushwhacker name o' Virgil Troaz, the outlaw I'm trackin'. Jones probably shoulda stayed back and found someone to keer for 'im insteda riding along with me to recover his own horse. But I take some blame too. I was hell bent for leather to catch up to the thief . . . had no time fer anything else.

"O.K., O.K." I said. "But let's care for him now."

six

LOUELLA TAKES CHARGE

*D*ublin's hide was tough. The raw spots responded to Louella's expert care. I watched as she toweled Dublin down and medicated his sore areas with a mixture that smelled of camphorated oil, and mint. Within minutes the big chestnut was contentedly munching hay.

I went to him and he turned his head to me. I stroked his neck and took my first good look at him.

He must have been very hungry, but he stopped eating as his big brown eyes gazed into mine and I saw something unusual there. Then he nuzzled me on my chest.

On my toes, close to his ear, I whispered, "forgive me, Dublin, you good old horse."

In response, Dublin nickered that same low sound, deep within him, just as when he'd come up from behind me back on the river.

He seemed to say, "It's O.K. Casey. It was just all in a day's work for me."

I realized that Dublin wasn't really old, just mistreated.

Then he gave me an affectionate bump with his nose and turned back toward his fodder. But before he took another mouthful, he looked at me again and nodded his big fine head. His beautiful eyes said, "don't fret."

The communication was unmistakable and I wiped away tears with my sleeve.

I sensed someone behind me.

A quiet voice said, "Dublin's a good, tough, horse. I've never seen a better comeback."

It was Louella. I couldn't turn to face her. I jerked off my bandanna and wiped my face.

"Yes, he's on the mend, thanks to you." I said hoarsely.

Dublin nickered. He swung his head in our direction and piece of hay flew into the air.

We both had to laugh.

I blew my nose to keep from sobbing and said, "Hey, Lou, I think we're having a three way communication here."

Lou smiled. "I know we are. I talk to our horses every day."

Then, turning to the horse, she stroked his neck. "Hey, there Dublin, we'll fix you up good as new."

"How many horses do you have here?"

"Five. A mare, two geldings and a colt."

"You ride much?" I asked, wanting to keep the light-hearted conversation going.

"Almost every day, after I run through the chores Tilly gives me to do."

"Tilly?"

"My mum. She's a good sort. Tending to Dublin has made us late for supper, but she's kept some warm for you and me."

Lou slowly handed me a towel and hesitated. "I've already washed up; meet you inside." In her wide-spaced blue eyes and pretty face, I read a change of heart . . . that maybe she'd been mistaken about me.

Minutes later I met Tilly and the two older sons. My brush with the outlaw had left me craving a good hot meal. The supper of turkey hash and gravy was plain, but there was lots of it . . . probably leftovers from Thanksgiving dinner.

Tilly Connor smiled as I wiped up the last bit with some tasty home made bread. I thanked the Connors for the meal and headed for the barn.

Wrapped in my heavy blanket, I drifted off, too exhausted to let a sore jaw keep me awake. The broken arm throbbed some, but the most troublesome ache was in my heart.

Sleep came quickly as I whispered, "Jasper, Jasper, will I ever see you again? Please God, help me to rescue him from Virgil Troaz."

I awoke at first light. TJ had saddled up and I rolled over just in time to see him leading the palomino into the paddock. With a twinge of regret, I heard them gallop off without me.

Last night when I saw Dublin's sore back, I knew it would be several days before he and I would ride again. So I just lay back and prayed that the feisty deputy would catch the outlaw and get Jasper back to me.

Later, when the sun streamed through the barn window, I rolled out to a chorus of cackling chickens.

My first thought was for Dublin. He was standing in his stall.

"Well, Dublin, how's my good horse this morning?"

I got a little thrill as he greeting me with a full whinny and several throaty sounds as I looked him over.

The raw spots appeared to be healing. In daylight I could see that the irritated areas across his back had lost their bright color and looked more normal. I brought him to the trough, then back in the stall, with one arm I managed to fork some hay to him.

Still feeling weak from my harrowing experience, I washed

up, ambled over and knocked at the Connor's back door.

Louella greeted me with a smile. "Come on in, Casey. Breakfast'll be ready in a jiffy."

Tilly Connor hailed me from the wood stove. "Good morning, young man. Hope the chickens didn't bother you none."

"Good morning Miz Connor. Chickens didn't bother me, I woke up when TJ left."

Bacon in the frying pan that Tilly tended sizzled up an appetizing aroma. A large blue serving plate sat warming on the sideboard. It was piled high with scrambled eggs and fried potatoes.

"Our men folk have already eaten," Tilly continued. "They're out pickin' the last of the field corn fer shuckin.'"

Over breakfast, I asked Louella if she had a favorite horse.

"Sure do," she said. "Merelda and I get along fine together. She's got spirit and loves heading up into timber country. Our favorite ride is down the road 'bout a mile, then we veer off into the pine and spruce that borders the Koreski's spread. We ride the wooded hillside clear to the ridge where I get the southeast view of the Wallowa Mountains."

"Sure like to take that ride some time."

Lou's eyes sparkled. "Maybe before you leave."

I turned to Mrs. Connor. "Ma'am, both my horse and I are a bit stove up just now. I need to speak to you and Mr. Connor about a room and board arrangement for a few days . . . just until I can head back home to Arborville."

"Well, young man," Tilly began. "We like to help out folks in need. Looks like you have been badly set upon."

"What you say is true, but I'd rest easier if I weren't leaning quite so heavily on your hospitality."

Just then, Mr. Connor came in through the back door.

"Good morning, Casey." He said.

"And a good morning to you."

"Have a good rest out there with the horses?"

"Yes, and I'm really enjoying this fine farm breakfast, too." I replied. "And that brings up my need to stay on here for a while if you are of a mind to have me."

"Well o'course." Mr. Conner said with a smile. "Feel free to stay on as long as you need to."

Out of the corner of my eye I noticed Louella break into a happy smile.

In a few words I expressed my thanks and suggested that I would be more comfortable if I could pay my way. Mr. Connor nodded in agreement. He sipped coffee and chatted with me as I finished my breakfast.

Mrs. Conner and Louella busied themselves with some large pans from the morning's milking.

I thought, "I'm not going to be much use around here; can't even help with the milking." And that thought brought up my broken arm, still in a crude splint. Louella seemed to read my mind.

"Say, Casey, that arm of yours should be put in a cast."

"Yes, I hadn't thought much about it."

Tilly came to Louella wiping her hands on her apron.

"Clear the table. Get the plaster. See to him."

Pleased that the Connors had agreed to some payment for their kindness to me, I watched in silence as Louella gently scissored the splint loose and sponged my arm with warm, soapy water.

I was somewhat taken aback by my black and blue arm. Louella read my expression and reassured me.

"Looks worse than it is. But it's a wonder you haven't had more pain with it."

I explained about how a geologist had come by to help.

"I think he did a good job of setting the bones." Louella

said knowingly. "Now I'll finish the job."

She mixed up a batch of Plaster of Paris with a wooden spoon, then tore a tea towel into strips.

Soon my arm was encased in a cast from my elbow to the tips of my fingers. As she put on the finishing touches, she looked up at me kindly.

"You don't want to be turning your wrist much while the bones are knitting."

Tilly slipped the last milk pan in the cooler and said proudly, "Lou wants to be a nurse."

"Thanks for tending to me, Louella, you'll make a mighty fine nurse."

"You're welcome, and call me Lou."

"O.K. Lou. On the way in, I checked out Dublin. He seems better this morning."

"Yes, earlier I sponged on more medication. He's healing and has such a lively spirit . . . I just feel good being around him."

"When do you think I'll be able to ride him again?" I asked.

Lou looked evasive. "Can't say yet. Maybe next week."

On one hand I was chompin' at the bit to get on the road again, but then, I couldn't help feeling a little flattered that Louella obviously liked having me around.

Faced with long days of inactivity, I desperately turned to the good farmer. "Mr. Connor," I began. "With this lame arm, I've never felt so worthless. I'm used to pulling my weight: milking, shoveling, pulling wire, chopping wood and riding herd. But if you'd permit it, there's one thing I can still do."

All three Connors stopped what they were doing and stared at me.

"I'm good at accounting. I might be helpful with your farm bookkeeping."

Tilly gave a little gasp, Mr. Connor put his hand to his mouth, and Lou beamed a wide smile, but none of them said a word.

I paused a few seconds, then left them speechless as I excused myself. "Well, it was just a thought. Thanks for breakfast. I'll go check on Dublin."

Dublin was fine. We exchanged a bit of gentle tenderness; I whispered in his ear while he nuzzled me. Then I sauntered out to have a look around.

The Connor's farm wasn't as grand and diversified as K2, but still impressive with large level fields of rich, loamy soil, and its pasture land. A sparkling creek ran along the back pasture. "This is just a nice, family farm." I thought.

At the far end I saw the two Connor boys picking corn and tossing the ears into a wagon.

I leaned on a fence post and watched two red-tailed hawks circling high overhead. A mile away I noted a tranquil scene; a neighboring farmer was burning dry grass in a ditch bank. The faint odor of smoke came to me and somehow added to the peace and contentment of just being there on a beautiful fall day.

I looked more closely at what income this place might produce. Would the corn crop, two cows and a few head of beef stock be enough to support a family of five? Was the farm free and clear of debt? If the Connors had hefty mortgage payments to make, they probably were in serious trouble.

Under my shirt I felt my leather wallet slung around my neck. No need to pull it out. I knew that it contained the spare cash put there for the trip south. Ten dollars would be a generous amount to leave in payment for Dublin and me when we left. If the Connors had a spare blanket and a few supplies for my trek back to Arborville, I'd insist on paying for those too. Otherwise, I'd stop at the first general store I could find.

seven

FISHING WITH ONE ARM

The sun was way to the west when I'd completed my circular stroll around the little ranch. I calculated it to be around two hundred acres. Entering the barn from the far end, which was filled with equipment, I came upon a steam tractor. Fascinated, I spent the rest of the afternoon looking it over.

As I bent over the compact boiler, I thought, "Well, this sure is a marvel of engineering . . . uses oil to fire this little boiler, then puts it right to work turning the rear wheels." My experiences with steam consisted of riding in a train pulled by a locomotive and working in a steam powered fishing boat.

Just then, one of the Connor boys I'd met yesterday walked in. "Hello, Fred." I began. "Just looking over your tractor."

"Ain't she a dandy! She's my Pop's pride and joy." Fred said glowing with pride himself. "We did away with the plow horses when Pop's brother, my Uncle Charlie, sold it to us 'couple of years ago . . . gave us a good, low price and threw in that corn grinder over there."

"Corn grinder? How does that work?" I asked.

Fred's face dropped. "Well, we've never quite figured that out."

Fred had to get on with tending the horses and, as I walked back to my spot in the barn, I found Louella looking after Dublin.

"Hello, Lou," I said cheerfully. "How's my favorite nurse?"

"Hi, Casey," she said, turning to me happily. "Where have you been today?"

"I walked a loop around your fine farm."

"Oh. Did you meet anyone on the way?"

"Just Fred, when I got back just now. He showed me the tractor."

"I wondered where you'd disappeared to. We missed you at mid-day meal."

Louella seemed thoughtful. "Casey, we were hoping that tractor would help our farm be more profitable, but it hasn't helped much. Truthfully, we're just barely making a go of it here."

"Sure sorry to hear that, Lou."

"Yes, and that's why Dad and Tilly didn't take you up on your offer to help with the bookkeeping . . . too proud to let you know about us."

"Umm. I understand, Lou. But even with just my short experience, I might be able to help some. You know, someone from the outside can take a fresh look at the situation and offer some advice . . . just a few changes might help."

Louella raised an eyebrow. "Like what, Mr. Washingtonian?"

"Well, just off the top of my head, I think I could get that corn grinder that your Uncle Charlie gave you up and running."

"Running? How?"

"I noticed a power take off shaft on that tractor your uncle put together."

"Take off?"

"Yes, it's just a continuation of the main shaft that sticks out in front a few inches. It has a link on it that can be attached to another piece of equipment."

"Could the tractor be used to run the corn grinder?"

"Haven't had time to check it out, but I think so."

"Casey! Dried corn is our main crop. Paying the folks at the grain elevator to grind it into meal and bag it is one of our biggest expenses!" Louella said excitedly. "Do you really think we could grind our own?"

"Next time I get a chance, we can find out for sure. In the meantime, I have a problem."

"What? Can I help?"

"Yes."

"How?" Louella took a step forward.

"Yesterday, the geologist gave me a bottle of liniment for my bruised left shoulder, but with the other arm in a sling, I can't rub it on."

Louella looked around. "Where's the bottle?" she asked eagerly.

"In my saddlebag."

A minute later, Louella had me resting on a bale of hay while she pulled back my shirt from my shoulder and gently rubbed on the soothing liniment. If she noticed the scars on my back from earlier injuries, she didn't mention it.

Even though my broken right arm still throbbed with a dull pain, thanks to Louella, at least my left shoulder felt much better. She had a way of not only healing a hurt, but sharing a sense of security.

That night as I lay awake in the hay trying to get to sleep, my arm with its uncomfortable cast, kept me awake. With an unsettled mind, Louella's pretty face loomed before me. My heart went out to the Connors . . . good, hard-working folks .

. . struggling to keep afloat financially.

After two or three hours, I got up and walked around. A cold, winter half-moon shone brightly and the bracing night air helped to clear my head. Why would the Connors feed a mare, two geldings and a colt? That many horses struck me as an unnecessary expense. I'd keep a team of two for the wagon with one doing double duty as a riding animal to tend the cattle. But then, Louella wouldn't have a horse of her own. I decided not to suggest selling a horse or two.

The Connors had no pigs. Raising hogs could really help with the food bill . . . they're cheap to feed and there'd be pork and bacon all year round.

I moved to Dublin's stall and the big fella raised his head with his usual horsy greeting. I stood for several minutes with my arm draped over his neck, and I felt my tension easing. As I moved away I knew that this was no ordinary animal. In some ways he had human instincts. Tonight when I'd felt worried about Jasper and concern for the Connors, Dublin had been there for me. When I returned to my blanket in the hay, I quickly relaxed into a deep sleep.

At sunup I washed the sleep from my eyes and looked up to see Mr. Connor. A good natured grin spread on his weathered face.

"Good morning, Casey. Do you suppose ya might feel up to walking over to where the creek widens out? I've found the trout fishing pretty good there."

Happy for the suggestion, I replied, "Well, yes. I never get as much fishing as I'd like."

"Well, if the rainbows are running good, you might even catch enough fer Tilly to fry up fer supper."

Mr. Conner quickly supplied me with fishing rod, reel, bait and a canvas creel for the catch. I walked out in bright sunshine to the bank of a beautiful wild stream and flipped a hook baited with an earthworm into the wide spot of the creek.

Sitting on a log I heaved a sigh of contentment. I thought, "The Connors may have their problems making ends meet, but they sure live in a beautiful part of the country."

An hour passed pleasantly. I watched hawks, this time flying low, hunting for field mice. Sparrows came by to check on me, chickadees flitted, flashing their wings in alder trees across the stream.

A pair of squirrels made regular round trips carrying acorns from the base of a large oak, hoarding food in a hollow place up in a cottonwood tree. A "V" formation of Canadian Geese flew over, honking as they went. The gurgling stream and a woodpecker's repeated rat-a-tat-tat were the only other sounds to be heard in the quiet of this beautiful spot. I observed many forms of wildlife, but no fish.

My outing by the brook passed pleasantly enough; a perfect way to kill time while arm and shoulder healed, but I didn't want to return without even one fish.

Well, if that happened, it would provide humility. I knew down deep that a humbling experience once in a while was good for the soul.

But just then, I heard a twig snap behind me and Louella joined me on the log. "Hello, Casey."

"Hi Lou, I suppose you came out to help me carry in all the fish I've caught." I chirped.

"Ha ha . . . fish not taking the bait, eh. Some days are like that."

Pleased to have her by me, I commented, "Didn't expect to see you out here."

"Well, I finished my chores early and came out to try my luck." With a flourish, she produced a pole and soon splashed a baited hook.

Louella looked over at my gear. "No luck with worms

today?"

"Lou, I've been here all morning and haven't even got a bite."

"Sometimes they'd rather have these waterbugs by the bank here. I just baited my hook with one."

Just then a large rainbow trout broke water as it took the hook. Louella skillfully let him run with it a bit before gently reeling him in.

"See! What did I tell you! They want waterbugs today," she said triumphantly holding up a flashing two-pounder.

The waterbugs were easy to catch, but while I switched bait and before I could cast it into the stream, I heard Louella call out: "Got another one!"

A bit slow with one arm, I finally got into position and flipped my baited hook out and expectantly watched it float downstream.

Louella dropped her second prize trout into her creel and promptly swung another baited hook upstream.

I held my breath to see which one of us would catch the next fish. She did. In an astonishing two minutes, Louella had caught three fine fish using waterbugs as bait.

But then it was my turn. While Louella baited up again, I finally got a trout on the line and it was a big one. I clutched my rod tightly.

Having realized that I'd be unable to reel in a catch one handed, I had used the lock button. This meant quite a jerk as, with a flash, the big rainbow came to the end of the line.

To compensate, I stood up and took a step forward. I certainly didn't want to lose my first fish of the day. A fighter, breaking water and jumping, he forced me to take another step, this time on a slippery rock. I fell forward up to my neck in icy water. Now I really wanted to land this fish. A little humbling goes a long way.

The thought of Louella showing off her three fine fish, and the spectacle of me, bedraggled, wet to the skin and with not one fish to show for the morning at the creek side, was more humility than I cared to experience.

Staggering up, I don't know which of us gyrated the most, me or the fish, but in the end, I gambled on a desperate move. I dropped the pole and lunged for the line. Thank God! I grasped it only a foot from the fish's mouth. On my knees, waist deep water, with the current buffeting me, I tried to pull the flailing fish toward shore, but fate intervened . . . my rod and reel caught between two rocks.

Fighting the current, I took a halting step backwards in an attempt to free the reel. But just then, I encountered Louella, who had waded in with the same idea of releasing the rod. As we both reached for it, I lost my balance.

I shouted, "Ohhhh!"

Then Louella, tried to grab my arm. "Omigosh!" she cried in dismay, toppling forward.

We both fell, with her on top of me. For a few agonizing seconds I thought I'd drown.

Neither of us could get traction on the slippery creek bed. We thrashed and floated together for several feet, with my lungs about to burst.

Louella pushed away and rose to her knees. Soon after I reared up sitting on the bottom gasping for air as the current threatened to drag me under again.

Easing our way to the shore we began to laugh. For several seconds, we rolled on the grassy embankment laughing uncontrollably. Wet to the skin, we were shivering from the cold, and I'd lost my fish. Still, we found the experience of floundering around in the creek together outrageously funny.

Our faces still contorted in laughter, we struggled to get serious. We had to get back.

Louella hastened to pick up her fishing gear and I carefully waded back in to retrieve mine.

Now the thought of catching nothing hit me. I was about to get skunked. Crestfallen, I stopped laughing. In spite of my heroic attempt to bring it in, I'd lost my beautiful rainbow trout.

Or had I? As I stepped in and picked up my pole, I felt a tug on the far end of the line. My fish was still on it! I let out a yell that could be heard for a mile!

"Yaaahooo!"

Chilled to the bone, but brimming with joy, I finally landed my fish.

Louella and I ran up to where she'd tethered Merelda. "Casey, we've got to get you home and put on a dry cast. Get up, we'll ride double."

With teeth chattering I gratefully agreed. "I'll r-ride b-b-behind. I'm g-going to have to h-hang on to you with my g-good arm."

Louella slung our gear on the side; we climbed into the saddle and headed for the farmhouse.

Mr. and Mrs. Connor greeted us when we rode in.

"Heavenly days, what have you two been up to?" Tilly exclaimed.

Mr. Connor laughed and slapped his knee. "Well, I hain't seen anything like this in a coon's age. Swimmin' in November can be a mite chilly."

Louella changed into dry clothes while Mr. Connor brought me into his bedroom and loaned me a pair of pants and a shirt. In minutes we were warming up by the kitchen stove.

It took several minutes for me to stop shivering while Louella brush-dried her long red hair. Then Tilly braided it at the kitchen table while Louella re-did my cast.

Tilly smiled at us. "Thanks you two, fer catchin' those fine trout fer our supper."

The Connors cracked up in merriment at my reply. "Well, Louella caught hers, but my trout kind of caught me."

I felt relieved and happy at the same time. I could have drowned out there.

eight

THE GRINDER

T he next morning at breakfast, Fred leaned over eagerly. "Casey, are you still lookin' to get the corn grinder a-workin'?"

"Yes, would you have time to look it over with me?" I asked.

"Sure would. How about just as soon as we finish here?"

I noticed the other Connors smiling their approval. Soon Fred and I were checking out the complicated piece of machinery.

"See here Casey, this big hopper's where you dump in the dried corn. This round part is 'spose to shuck the kernels off and discard the cobs. Then the corn goes into the grinder section here. The corn meal comes out this spout in front where it can be bagged."

"O.K., I'm beginning to see how it works," I said. "There's an adjustment dial here with three positions: fine, medium and coarse."

Fred and I pushed the grinder over to the steam tractor. "Look, these two connections match up," Fred said with excitement.

"But we need a way to connect them."

Fred's eyes got big. "I think we have what we're lookin' for sittin' on the shelf. It came with the grinder."

A minute later, Fred slipped a new, two foot tubular shaft out of its box.

It was my turn to show excitement.

"Skidoo, Fred! This connecting shaft comes with a universal joint on either end. Without them, we'd need to match up the shafts exactly, and even then there'd be no good way to tie them together."

While I connected up the grinder to the tractor, Fred pushed a wagonload of corn over to the hopper and hooked it up to a rope and pulley hoist suspended from the ceiling.

Next, Fred began to pull on the rope and the back of the wagon lifted off the ground. Hundreds of dry ears of corn fell into the hopper. We were almost ready to give the operation a trial run.

Fred excitedly fired up the tractor while I ran to find Mrs. Connor. We needed cotton bags that we could fill with corn meal if the grinder worked. I found her on the back porch with an armload of sacks.

"I thought you might be needing these if you got that contraption to workin'."

"You're a step ahead of me, Mrs. Connor."

Then, after handing over the cotton sacks, Mrs. Connor offered me a bushel basket.

"What's this for?" I asked.

"When you get to grinding, catch the first batch in the basket," the wise farm wife suggested. "I figure it'll taste of dust with a machine flavor. I'll feed it to the chickens."

"I wouldn't have thought of that, Mrs. Connor."

"Well, I'll use meal from your second batch for some cornbread. It'll go good with what we're havin' fer supper. I'm a fixin' up a big pot of chili."

Fred and I spent most of the afternoon working on the grinding project. The first change came even before we began to grind.

We found that the shed was filling with exhaust fumes and Fred leaped into the driver's seat and carefully backed the tractor with grinder attached out into the open. At that point, Mr. and Mrs. Connor, older son Ezra, and Louella all came out to watch. What a joy it was pull the 'start' lever and see the fresh cornmeal fill one cotton sack after another.

The grinder's last stage sewed the top of each bag shut with cotton thread. The Connors could hardly control their excitement. They walked around and chattered above the sound of the grinding. Louella and Tilly took over filling and sewing one bag after another.

The project was a big success . . . including the lip smacking delicious cornbread and chili supper that concluded an afternoon of satisfying farm labor. Later, as I sipped coffee with Mr. Connor in the parlor, we chatted a bit.

"Now, son," he began. "You say you were brought up in the big city, but seein' you warm up to the job, I'd judge that they's a heap o' good ol' dirt farmer in you."

"Thanks, I take kindly to that. Actually I enjoy farm work, especially when I have two healthy arms."

"You should. It takes a lot o' solid effort to make a go of it, but farm life is mostly pretty darn good."

"I've observed that myself."

"It's true. And today you've made it even better for us." Mr. Connor said as he took another sip from his steaming mug.

"Casey, we shoulda got that grinder a goin' fer ourselves, but it took you to give us the push and supply just the right touch with it."

That evening Louella and I sat on the back porch and

watched the sun set through the trees. As the dappled gold rays spread across the valley, shadows lengthened, a new and very pleasant sense of contentment came over me. The soft hooting of an owl came from a stand of cottonwoods. The pleasant odor of the fields as they lay fallow, mingled with a touch of wood smoke. How different from the sights and sounds of the big city! I loved it. If it weren't for missing Jasper, I'd have felt perfect, blissful happiness.

Louella looked at me warmly. "Casey, you did a very good thing for us today. I know that Papa already thanked you, but we all appreciate getting us set up to grind our own corn."

I returned her gaze, "I'm pleased to find a way to repay, at least in part, for the kindness you've showered on me, Lou."

Louella went on. "On top of everything else, you speak so well too. Casey, I've come to admire you in many ways." Now looking a bit sad, she asked, "What is it like at the big K2 ranch?"

That really got me started, and for the next five minutes or so, I spoke of the fine folks in Arborville, both at Overton Manor and out on the ranch.

"From what you say, I'd like to meet the Kinsman family that you are a part of," Louella said.

"I think you'd like them, especially Annie, Colette and Neva. Neva is about our age."

"And the three girls are your cousins?" Louella asked with a raised eyebrow.

"I certainly thought they were."

"You mean they aren't? That sounds so strange."

I turned and looked directly at Louella. "Lou, a few weeks ago I was talking to my mom and she told me that when she was a child, the Kinsmans adopted her as one of their own."

Louella opened her mouth, but nothing came out.

"Well, if you're surprised, so was I. Although they treat

my mom and me as genuine family, we are not Kinsmans by blood."

Louella looked down at her hands. "Casey, excuse me for asking, but might you have some feelings for Neva or the others? Beyond that of cousins, I mean."

"Well, yes, I guess I do. But there's still a problem with that."

"I can't imagine what it would be? Don't the girls know about your mom?"

"You're sharp, Lou. That's exactly the case. The girls still think of me as a first cousin."

"Well, Land o' Goshen, why don't you just come right out and tell 'em."

"I wanted to do that, but when I asked Mom about it, she said to wait. She said, 'The right time will present itself.'"

"I suppose she's right. There must be a reason for her wanting to wait."

"I think it might have to do with the fact that both my mom and I lived in New York up until about a year ago. She might feel that we should take a bit more time to get established in Arborville before the subject of our relationship comes up."

"She might feel self-conscious about either of you being the one to announce it. If it came out through any other source she might welcome it," Louella guessed.

"Lou! I'll say it again. You're sharp!" I exclaimed. "That really rings true."

Just before we left the subject, I began to think that there must be some indirect way to let folks know about my true Kinsman family relationship.

"Lou, may I come back to the subject of your fine farm here."

"Of course. What other magical scheme might you have up your sleeve? Something from the Broadway stage perhaps?"

Louella said airily.

"Ha! Ha. Not unless they've put the Three Little Pigs into production."

"Pigs?" Louella pursed her mouth. "Pigs! I'll bet you're going to suggest we begin to raise some smelly porkers."

"Now Lou, here I am the city guy coming off as a 'know it all,' but doggone it, I do think you folks might consider it."

Louella smirked and really looked amused. "Go on. I'm listening."

"I'm thinking hog raising on a small scale. You could have a shed built on the back of the barn, out of the way. Pigs do wallow in mud some, but they actually keep their manure separate. They're smarter than most people think." I hesitated, regretting now that I brought up the subject.

With a "Umm humm," Louella kept smiling, so I bumbled on.

"They could be cheap to feed. Certain times of the year, you could let them out to forage and I'll bet there's a German butcher around here somewhere that would cut and cure hams and bacon for you, smoke sausages too."

Louella continued to smile so I went on.

"You know Lou, I just wanted to give a little free advice." Lou just stared at me.

"I'll be leaving soon." I added lamely.

I finished with: "Sometimes free advice is worthless."

At that, Lou burst out laughing. "Casey, you are really full of hot air sometimes, but I love it."

I could feel my face getting hot; I knew I was blushing.

Well, I'd really overdone it. Helping to get the grinder going was one thing, but my hog raising suggestion, well, THAT is what Uncle Harry would probably call being "insufferably patronizing." Now I had a real chance to practice humility.

"Well, I just made a total fool of myself didn't I?"

"Yes, but it just kind of fits with your suggestion about helping with our bookkeeping."

"That was out of line wasn't it."

Louella's smile was gone. "Yes, way out."

"If I get up and bend over, will you kick me?" I said half seriously.

"Casey, don't tempt me. If you didn't have a broken arm, I'd take you up on it."

I thought fast, "My broken arm didn't stop you from socking me on the jaw."

Louella wasn't smiling now. "At the time, I thought you had it coming."

After a pause of a few seconds, I came out with, "Sorry, I've been so full of myself and talked down to you . . . spoiled our time out here. Guess there's only one thing left to say right now . . . good night."

I started to leave, but Louella said, "Wait." Then she leaned over and gave me a light kiss on the jaw. "That's for socking you on the first day."

Her smile was back. "Keep doing good things. Your heart's in the right place."

Then with a "So long, Casey," she slipped away.

Such misery! My shoulder was stiffening up due to my work on the grinder. Now I'd ruined my chance to have Louella apply some liniment. But worse, I felt pangs of remorse about overstepping myself. I'd been puffed up with pride and I'd paid a price for it. I'd put my foot in my mouth. If only I'd left well enough alone!

Then I thought of Mr. Lambrusco's advice. "It doesn't help to say, if only. Life is the best teacher. Learn from your mistakes and look ahead."

I wandered toward the barn, then stopped dead in my tracks. In the gloom of dusk, a man came down the driveway walking his horse.

Suddenly all else was forgotten as I recognized Deputy Torgeson.

I called out. "Hi there, T.J."

TJ looked trail weary. Bursting with curiosity, I waited for him to check in with Mr. Conner and tend to his horse.

As he dressed down the palomino, he told a sad tale.

"I lost Troaz's trail only a mile further down. Shoulda stopped then and there, but went all the way down to a little place called Huntington, near the border. I asked around and nobody'd seen the rider on yer hoss."

That was bad news. "Did you pick out any three diamond marks on the trail?"

"Down the road a ways a buncha wagon tracks come on. Didn't see the diamonds after that."

TJ looked me in the eye, "Trackin' an outlaw into Oregon's one thing. We got 'ciprocal agreement here. Coulda gone on another day or two into I-dee-ho, but that's too far outa my jurisdiction."

TJ turned and headed for the kitchen. "The way that no account wuz ridin,' I figure yer hoss'll wind up in San An-tone, Texas."

I didn't want to hear that Jasper might be galloping out of my life. When I hadn't seen Jasper come in with TJ, I'd expected the worst. Still, I refused to give up hope. Tomorrow after early breakfast, I'd head southwest. I trusted TJ's ability as a professional lawman, but for my own peace of mind, I had to see for myself if the three diamond trail had been completely trampled out.

With Fred's help, I scribbled a left-handed telegram to the Kinsmans and addressed it to Uncle Harry at the Arborville depot. In a few words, I tried to reassure everybody that I'd received the best treatment from some farm folks and that I'd be heading back home as soon as I was able.

When TJ came into the barn to bed down, I asked him to send my note and he agreed saying, "I'll make it a part of my report."

I got up before TJ, washed, combed my hair, and was soon enjoying a bowl of oatmeal with brown sugar and cream. As I wolfed down two thick pieces of cornbread heavily spread with huckleberry jam, I thought. "This extra is for the road."

I sipped a cup of Tilly's steaming hot coffee, and told her of my plan to trace Jasper's trail as far as I could before heading back to K2.

"I'll pray for your safe return home. We're all going to miss havin' you around, Casey. Jeb and I, Ezra and Fred, we've liked you bein' with us . . . you're just good company."

"Thanks Mrs. Connor. I feel right at home here . . . wish I could stay longer."

"You are welcome to come back and visit fer as long as you like. You don't need an excuse, but in the spring you might want to check in and see how your grinder idee paid off for us."

"Well, now. That is a dandy thought."

Tilly refilled my cup and sat down with me. "Now let's talk about Lou."

I'd noticed earlier that she hadn't mentioned Louella among those who'd miss me. I eagerly waited for what would come next.

Tilly took a sip of her coffee. "Louella is kinda broken up about you leavin'." Reacting to the surprised look on my face, she went on.

"She told me that she gave you a 'lash of the whip' last night . . . about you overplayin' your advice to us."

"Well, Mrs. Connor, she leveled with me and I needed to hear it. Sometimes the truth hurts."

"You were just tryin' to help us, Casey. She knows that."

"I see . . . she did it for me."

Tilly smiled. "No, she did it for herself. She was gettin' too attracted to someone who was about to up and leave her."

"I don't get it. How did straight-talking me help her?"

"You're young, Casey. You've got a lot to learn about women. She couldn't come out and tell you how she really felt, so she picked on you."

I sat stunned for a few seconds. At that moment I forgot about Jasper, K2 and everybody else. I just wanted to stay here on this beautiful farm with these great people. I especially wanted to be with Louella . . . go riding with her up in the mountains, chat on the porch, watch the sun set, go fishing again. Oh! What a tug on my heart!

I sat digesting both my fine breakfast and these new thoughts, when Mr. Connor joined us.

After the usual morning greetings, Tilly realized that I needed to get going.

"Jeb," she suggested. "Casey wants to get an early start on the trail. Why don't you saddle up Dublin fer him while I'm fixin' your breakfast."

As we parted, I thanked Tilly for everything and she handed me a sack of food for later.

"Come back and see us now, ya hear!" she said, and despite the cast, she gave me a long hug and a kiss on the cheek.

As Mr. Connor saddled up Dublin, he paused. "Besides givin' Dublin another dressing down yesterday," he said. "Lou washed and scrubbed his saddle blanket and cleaned up the saddle and bridle too."

I noticed that Dublin was healing nicely and now he looked sharp, too. But still, I made a mental note to take it easy on him in the days to come.

"Well, young fella," Mr. Connor began, while giving me a left-handed hand shake. Sure has been a pleasure havin' you with us."

When I tried to pay him for all the hospitality, he refused. "We can't take anything fer you bein' with us. You're like family."

Pleased to find that I could easily mount up on my own, I parted with a wave. "Say so long to the boys . . . and to Louella."

nine

JASPER'S COLD TRAIL

I had little hope of picking up Jasper's trail as I turned southeast, but kept Dublin to a walk for the first mile or so.

I was heartened to see an occasional diamond mark still visible. Then came the crossroads TJ had mentioned; several car and wagon tracks canceled Jasper's trail. We ambled on for another few hundred feet to be sure no trace of Jasper's hoof marks remained.

Now I sensed the full weight of my lost horse. I felt it in the pit of my stomach as I patted Dublin on the neck. "No point going any farther, boy. We've no way to track Jasper."

Then, with a low whinny, Dublin did a curious thing. As we reared around, jogged back, he veered off at a sign that read: THE OLD OREGON TRAIL.

I'd read about the Oregon Trail and was overcome with awe at traveling where some 100,000 pioneers had gone before. Two of Mr. Lambrusco's books had offered fascinating background.

Oh! How I respected those pioneers with their wagons and belongings, risking their lives and enduring hardship to build a new life for themselves in the Oregon Territory, the land where dreams of a prosperous family life could come true.

In addition to Oregon, this new land included what would become Washington and British Columbia. At the time, it spread from California clear up to the Russian territory of Alaska and its attraction to settlers spurred a huge western migration.

Early on, several foreign nations had vied with the United States for control of this vast territory. They made claims tied to explorers and early settlers in the region. But Mr. Conner told me that, after most claims had been settled, it actually came down to the threat of war between United States and England over the Canadian boundary. Then, in 1844, the dispute was settled peacefully by treaty.

Most of the pioneers who had traveled the Oregon Trail had been heading for the beautiful Willamette Valley, south of Portland, Oregon.

Now, Dublin and I traveled a short distance on the famous trail. Then, Dublin suddenly took off on a narrow roadway.

Astonished at Dublin again taking the lead, I continued to give him his head, and we ambled on and on. Farmland gave way to hill country. Soon, in bright sunshine now, we entered tall timber. Dublin cantered on, up a faint trail into the wooded area of the Blue Mountains.

Shafts of sunlight warmed the woods. Problems and pains forgotten, I matched Dublin's smooth motion; we floated freely, timelessly, through thick forest. My hat slipped back and the cool pine-scented breeze tickled my nose and ruffled my hair.

A chill of happy excitement flooded through me as two chipmunks scampered up a pine tree and a large pinecone dropped and bounced nearby.

I closed my eyes and gave myself over to the magical moment. My spirit took wing. Dublin became the mythical Pegasus as upwards we soared to God's transcendent realm and I touched the edge of eternity. Beyond time and distance, we journeyed on into nature's untrespassed wilderness.

Then, Dublin gave out a long neigh and slowed to a walk.

I came back with a start. There, just ahead, stood a man of medium build in a dark hat and a long leather cape. He held a rifle waist high, pointed at my head. Beyond lay a log cabin, and two outbuildings.

"Get down!" He said firmly.

My heartbeat shot up as I dismounted and put Dublin's reins into the man's outstretched hand. I noted with alarm, his black beard, dark staring eyes, and long hair, tied in back.

Dublin snorted a greeting, and nuzzled the man with the same affectionate nickering sound he'd had for me. And I was stunned by what it meant.

This man had knocked me off Jasper! Standing before me is the bushwhacker that TJ is after! This is the notorious Virgil Troaz!

And, OF COURSE! Dublin brought me here, because HE LIVES HERE. DUBLIN IS THE OUTLAW'S HORSE!

Noting the cast on my right arm, Virgil Troaz said, "Put your hand on your head and walk ahead of me." He motioned me into a small stable. I looked around for my horse, and thrilled to the sight of Jasper's K2 saddle, blanket, and bridle slung over a rack by a stall.

I thought, "Skidoo! Jasper's here!" But then fear hit. The worst had happened.

In seconds, the outlaw wound a thin rope around my arms and cinched it up in back. Then pushing me down to the dirt floor, he tied my ankles.

The outlaw glared at me. "Don't get ideas about trying to

escape back down the trail," he said, brandishing the rifle. "It's a long way on foot to the main road. I'd catch you . . . shoot you dead before you got half a mile."

With that, he shut and bolted the door from the outside.

Deeply depressed and discouraged, lying on bare ground, I began to feel the penetrating cold of the mountain. But I fought off despair. After all, Jasper was nearby, not in some far away place. So long as I was alive there was hope, but I knew that I must get free right now.

The ropes that bound my ankles were so tight my toes were already beginning to get numb, but those binding my arms, weren't as constricting. When Virgil had wound the rope around my arms and chest, like a horse being cinched up, I'd taken a big breath. When I exhaled, the ropes gave me some wiggle room.

It took me a few minutes to work my left hand free. That gave me a chance to get hold of the knife Cal Paluskin had given me. I'd strapped its sheath to my leg just inside my boot. Curling my legs back, I pulled out the knife and cut the rope, freeing my ankles. Now I sat up and turned the blade around cutting the upper ropes as well.

Thank God! Now I had a chance to escape.

From a crack in the wall I could see two horses in the small corral. For days, my eyes had longed to see the vision of my beautiful horse and now, there was Jasper, only a few feet away, contentedly cropping grass with Dublin.

I moved away in frustration. I felt like bumping my head against the wall but held back for fear of making any sound. Even if I could somehow get Jasper in here without a bridle to lead him, I still wouldn't be able to saddle him up with a broken arm.

No! I had to get out of this shed and make a run for it. Now!

Sticking the point of my knife through the crack of the door, I worked the outside bolt back.

Outside, I noticed Dublin's saddle and bridle draped on a rail under cover of the eave. I'd have to go it on foot. But I got a break. Dublin's saddlebag with food and canteen inside had been carelessly hung on the hitching rail. I scooped it up and scampered across the clearing on my way back down the trail.

ten

THE CHASE

*T*he escape had to follow a plan. First, pacing myself would be important to conserve strength. I set a steady trot instead of wildly racing down the trail. Next, I'd jump into the underbrush if I sensed movement or heard a horse behind me.

The sun, barely visible through the tall evergreens, had begun to follow its downward arc. I had to get started. But how far on this trail had I come to get here? I'd been in a state of reverie, unaware of time and distance. Did I have five miles to go back? Ten?

Downward I jogged until, gasping for air, I collapsed on a pile of pine boughs. How long would it be before Virgil discovered my disappearance? I'd remembered to close and bolt the shed door. There was satisfaction in that. Those simple actions might buy me some time.

Before I resumed my steady dash down the hill, I paused, thrust my knife into the earth, put my ear on the ground and with teeth clamped on its handle, listened carefully. Cal had taught me this clever way to detect footsteps within a fairly wide area. I was relieved to hear nothing.

But, to use an old adage, "I wasn't out of the woods yet."

In this desperate attempt to escape, my mind took over, calculating my rate of descent.

I judged each of my downhill strides to be roughly a yard. I jogged at about two of them, or 6 feet, a second . . . multiplied by 60 seconds was 360 feet a minute. Judging ten minutes of jogging and allowing for rest breaks, I could run about half a mile in ten minutes.

If I could keep up the pace, I could run about three miles in an hour. I was cheered by this. There should be enough daylight for me to run down to a farmhouse, or to the crossroads where I could get help from a passerby.

I imagined a stopwatch in my head. It was easy for me to visualize the sweep second hand and count the minutes too.

But after two, ten minute jogs, I realized that my calculations were for ideal conditions. Sitting on a log, catching my breath, I judged that I had traveled about a mile.

But the exertion had taken its toll. My broken arm had left me low on energy. Getting down off the mountain by sunset was unrealistic. I began to look around for a place to spend the night.

It was time to take stock. I'd been stalked once by a man determined to kill me . . . a living nightmare I'd barely survived, I vowed to do better if Virgil Troaz came after me.

The saddlebag might prove to be a lifesaver. Inside I found the small canteen and took three sips of water. Next I feasted my eyes on the four turkey sandwiches and four hard-boiled eggs in kind Tilly's lunch sack.

About to replace the precious food in the saddlebag, a note dropped out. It was from Louella. It read:

Dear Casey,

I'll probably be doing the milking when you

leave us, so I thought I'd better write a goodbye note.

Your stay with us was too brief. Maybe you can visit us

in the spring and I can give you another fishing lesson. (smile)

I pray that you will find your horse and return to your home safely. Lou

Louella! I'd thought that she hadn't even cared enough to say goodbye to me. Pleased beyond words, I slipped the note into my shirt pocket.

Rested now, I jogged another ten minutes. I stopped, and just at the same instant that I bent down to place the saddlebag on the trail, I heard a whine and thud of a bullet hitting the tree just in front of me. The delayed crack of a rifle followed and echoed again and again. Virgil Troaz was on my trail and had almost put a bullet through my head!

Relived to be alive, I tingled all over. I got my second wind and sped down a curved section of the trail. Since sound travels at roughly one thousand feet a second, the first shot had to have been made from over a thousand feet back. I also knew that I had to outsmart my pursuer or the next shot would put an end to me.

Out of sight in the bend of the trail, I stopped, reached down, broke a few ferns to the left of the trail to throw Virgil off the track. Then, for twenty feet, I retraced my steps backwards, careful to put each foot down in exactly the same place before taking a large step off the trail to the right. If I'd done it right, Virgil might think that I'd left the trail on the other side and some thirty feet farther on.

Praying that my diversion would work, I picked my way up the slope searching for a place to hide. And some two hundred paces farther on, I saw a hillside with an opening in it. A cave, partly hidden behind a clump of fern.

Placing my toes on rocks, cones and tree limbs, so as not to leave tracks, I quickly entered the mouth of the cave, and on hands and knees, crawled on in a ways. Now I could stretch out and catch my breath.

Terrified, I heard a slight rustle behind me. I detected a strange, stale odor. I was not alone in the cave!

My first thought was of a hibernating bear. What had Cal taught me about them? Right! Leave them alone! If aroused from their long winter's sleep, they'd be in a very cranky mood. My imagination conjured up a vision of being horribly chewed and clawed to death.

But then, with my heart still pounding from the close call on the trail, I squelched the urge to bolt out into the woods where Virgil was searching for me.

After a minute I gingerly put my hand out behind me and felt the coarse hair of the big animal. It was much closer than I'd thought! Thank God I hadn't stumbled into it in the dark.

I held my breath and listened. Yes! I could hear slow breathing.

With the hair on the back of my neck standing up in fear, I began to shake . . . but not from cold. I was terrified. I slowly inched back toward the cave opening and noticed that just inside to the left, it broadened out some. I crept into this hollowed space, and was pleased to find a pile of big vine maple leaves. "Probably wafted in by the wind," I thought.

Exhausted, I cushioned my head on the saddlebag, covered myself with leaves and remembered no more 'til early morning.

Suddenly I was awake!

Had I heard the sound of a horse neighing down on the trail? Yes . . . another neigh followed and throaty sounds too. It was Dublin! The determined outlaw was looking for me and would probably investigate this cave as a likely hiding spot near where my footprints had ended.

My fears became reality as I heard Dublin coming closer, his big hooves breaking twigs.

I leaned forward slightly and caught sight of Virgil as he dismounted, and approached rifle in hand.

"Hey!" he yelled. "I know you're in there! Come out! Come out or I'll blast you out."

I guessed he was bluffing because I hadn't seen him check the ground for my footprints. I started to reach for my knife, but had no plan of action. In my cramped position, it would be awkward to crawl out, rise up and attack.

If I tried to resist, Virgil would pull the trigger and this time there'd be no sound lag. Just then I heard the ear-splitting crack of his rifle.

My pursuer yelled at the top of his voice, "That was a warning shot in the air. Next time I'll pump five rounds in there. You won't stand a chance!"

Near panic I decided to surrender. I might have a small chance of surprising him with my knife.

Virgil shouted, "I'll count to three! ONE! TWO!"

I cried, "WAIT!" but was drowned out by a deafening roar.

The mammoth monster behind me had been roused from a deep sleep and was in foul temper. Eyes blazing, lips curled with teeth and claws ready to tear its tormenter to shreds, it dashed past my hiding space directly at an astonished Virgil, who quickly fired.

The shot went wild, but the crack of the rifle seemed to enrage the bear even more.

The bear lunged, and with a powerful swipe, sent Virgil's rifle flying as the terrified outlaw scrambled away, ducking behind a slim birch tree.

The bear lunged again, its momentum carrying it through the tree, snapping it off at the base. Then the behemoth, slowed only slightly by entangling birch branches, roared on. Virgil sped back toward a waiting Dublin.

Virgil ran for his life; frantically leaping on Dublin with the furious bear barely inches behind. The savvy horse rocketed from a standstill to a gallop in one second or less with the bear in hot pursuit, its bellows of rage mixing with Virgil's high-pitched exhortations to Dublin, "Giddyap! Giddyap! Giddyap!"

But Dublin needed no such encouragement and obviously outran the fierce wild animal for I heard no screams from on down the hill.

Fighting the urge to run, I decided to stay put in my snug, hiding place. I didn't want the big animal to return and take off after me.

Within a few minutes, the huffing bear, snuffing and still emitting whining growls, came lumbering back. When it came by, my hair stood up in fear as it swung its huge head and beady red eyes in my direction. In the gloom of the cave's recess, logic told me I couldn't be seen, but I almost died of fright when the bear let out a big "SNUFF," snorting a stench of stale breath in my face, before retreating back to its lair.

Throughout the attack, I'd not moved a muscle. Now, with the immediate danger gone, I needed to change my cramped position. Still too scared to move, I held out for another ten minutes before slowly, very slowly, inching my way to the mouth of the cave.

"Skidoo!" I thought, as I took deep lungfulls of the fresh mountain air. "How great to be alive after cheating death again."

I had survived the latest crisis and felt a surge of relief as the stiffness from my cramped position began to ease. I limbered up as I strode down the trail once more. On the way, I picked up the outlaw's rifle.

What should I do next? I ran in a cloud of doubt.

Virgil, a shrewd mountain man, would suspect I was behind him . . . no more rushing headlong down toward the crossroads for me. What had begun as a race, was now a chess match. If I were to survive, I must outwit Virgil. Without his rifle, he would logically lie in wait, hoping to jump me.

Then I thought, "High ground! Find a place where I can command a view of the surrounding area."

Trotting down the trail now, I desperately sought a vantage point and, as I came to a straight stretch, caught sight of one. Up a rocky slope of scattered scrub oak, an outcrop with a rocky overhang looked to be the perfect mountain retreat.

In minutes, I'd seated myself comfortably out of sight, with a clear view of the area below where I could spot anyone on the trail for at least fifty yards in either direction.

Now breakfast was in order. I was famished but I held myself to one sandwich, an egg and one of the apple cinnamon cookies also packed by kind Tilly. I saved the rest for what might become a long test of wills in the open with Virgil. The canteen, though small, was still almost full.

I decided I'd have to wait out the day, and, if necessary, the night too.

On my trudge up the slope, I'd noticed a dozen deer up ahead but had paid little attention to them. But now, my scalp prickled as I spotted the largest cat I'd ever seen, stealthily stalking a doe.

I'd heard the eerie scream of the cougar in the far reaches of the K2 ranch, and had come across their large paw prints, but had never actually seen one of the huge animals.

Staring in shocked fascination, my heart began to thump as the huge cat suddenly sprang on its prey. It caught the doe by the neck and killed it with one powerful shake that lifted the smaller animal entirely up into the air before dropping it in a rumpled heap on the grassy forest floor.

As I watched, the cougar began to feast on its kill. Half an hour later, filled with its favorite food, the two hundred pound cat wandered up the slope, its large yellow eyes gleaming satisfaction. And I couldn't believe it . . . the fierce feline was making its way up to me in my rock-covered hiding place. I reached for the rifle but thought better of it. Nothing would bring Virgil to me more quickly than the sharp crack of his rifle.

Once again, I gambled by doing nothing. If the cougar came all the way in to me, I resolved not to move. I knew that these huge beasts were not known for attacking humans. With its full stomach, it probably was looking for a secluded place to relax. It found such a place under my rock ledge.

The cat, easily reaching nine feet from nose to tail, not only decided to share my hiding place, it stretched out within an arms length of me.

A thrill of terror tingled all the way down to my toes. I shivered from the chill air but mostly from fear as the cougar curled its three-foot long tail around itself and gazed directly at me. I was so scared I couldn't move. For several minutes we just stared at each other. Finally with a feline lick of its chops, the cat closed its eyes and began to purr.

The next half an hour passed quietly as I tried not to move a muscle. The totally unexpected purring didn't relieve my fear. I could imagine a sudden flare of temper, as one of those huge paws, claws extended, lashed out at me for disturbing the peace.

Then I heard the familiar sound of Dublin's nickering down the trail.

I peeked down the trail and sure enough, there was Troaz, who seemed to be looking up at me. Could he see me through the brush between us? No! Troaz was looking up at the cougar, which at that very moment, had raised its huge head and was glaring back down at the horse and rider.

Dublin nervously let out a snort and shook his head. Troaz continued to stare wide-eyed as he quietly rode on by. Minutes later, my cougar yawned and put its head down again. Seconds later it began to snore.

Unbelievable! Back in Brooklyn, Mr. Lambrusco had said, "Truth can be stranger than fiction."

The strange behavior continued. When I stretched out from my cramped position, the cougar rolled over and snuggled against me.

No longer fearful of this friendly cougar, I began to enjoy its pleasant, wild smell and the intimacy of its furry, warm body next to me and I had to fight to stay awake.

My cougar's snoring was so reassuring that I actually dozed off myself. If I lived through this ordeal who would ever believe my story? Napping with a cougar while being stalked by a desperate outlaw? Pretty far fetched stuff!

My nap was brief, lasting but a few minutes. I awoke with a start as I realized that I was cuddling up with a cougar.

Now was the time for me to disengage and head down the hill again. With Virgil back up the trail, I could resume my measured march to the crossroads . . . so why push my luck here?

But I moved away cautiously. As I rolled away from my cougar, I feared the worst. But the big cat was in such a deep state of slumber that I was safe to leave and head down the trail.

After my first ten-minute jog, I stopped for a break and took a sip of water. I repeated this routine for the next hour and began to feel that I might finally break free from Virgil Troaz's threat.

Finally I collapsed on a grassy mound. Gasping for breath, I took a little longer break this time. I sipped from the canteen and took in my surroundings. I saw nothing suspicious, so I moved on. But first I made a momentous decision. The heavy rifle was slowing my stride . . . I tossed it into a stand of underbrush.

In my new life at K2, I'd felt at home with every aspect of it . . . except for guns. I was a westerner by birth, if not by upbringing in New York, but I had avoided taking up with handguns, rifles or shotguns. They all had played an important part in the era of pioneer survival. But that was in the developing west. I wasn't akin to that now.

I reasoned that if Virgil suddenly came upon me out here, I would be faced with defending myself, but now with him behind me, I could hide the gun in the brush.

What a relief!

But the cagey outlaw wasn't behind me. He'd slipped back on the trail below, passing my cougar and me as we'd napped. He'd obviously been watching from a hiding place. At the next turn in the trail, as fate would have it, just after I'd ditched the gun, he suddenly appeared from behind a cedar and jumped me.

I had kept alert all along. As Virgil stepped out to club me, I reacted. Dodging away as he swung an oak limb at my head, I threw off the sling that held my heavy plaster cast.

Now in a fight for my life, and exhausted from my long run, I summoned the strength of desperation to ward off my attacker.

Virgil whipped out his knife and lunged. He was strong and wiry, but I was quick.

I faded back, crouched, and, all in one motion, rose up with my knife in hand to take a swipe at Virgil's arm as he recovered his position. I had expected only to intimidate him, but the tip of my weapon actually jabbed the underside of Troaz's coat sleeve.

With a cry of surprise, the outlaw lunged again, and I instinctively used my cast as a shield deflecting his long shiny blade.

Furious, but wary, Troaz sprang again. I dodged back, slashing at his arm, and my knife penetrated his coat at the elbow. He paused for an instant, grabbing his arm.

Despite jabbing him twice, I sensed I would lose this fight if I didn't attack. I whirled away and came back around full circle with my right arm extended in a roundhouse swing. And I connected. With every bit of strength I had left, I bashed him on the side of his head with my plaster club. Taken by surprise, Virgil's hat flew off and he went down.

Louella's cast had provided me with a secret weapon that turned out to be quite useful in my time of need. Her handiwork had done the job well. Virgil lay unconscious; face down amid a clump of bear grass.

With a pounding heart I pried the fallen man's knife from his hand. In the tradition of mortal combat, I should have put an end to him then and there, killing him with his own weapon.

Despite the pain he'd caused me, though, I just couldn't do that. Instead, I secured his arms behind him with his belt. I figured that he'd get free, but it was the best I could do one-handed.

Again, with the idea of slowing him down, I took time to pull his boots off and threw them as far as possible down into the gully below.

I looked for Dublin. Tethered some fifty yards away, he gave me his usual horsy welcome. Now finally, I'd ride the rest of the way.

What a comfort it was to once again enjoy a swift ride on horseback! I relaxed a little and began to think ahead.

Certainly before nightfall I'd ride into the farmyard at the Connor farm. I'd enlist their aid to return here, capture Virgil and retrieve Jasper. For the first time, I could see the end of this saga that had begun a week before on the banks of the Columbia.

eleven

VIRGIL'S REVENGE

*A*s I continued to return to a normal awareness of things, my broken arm began to throb with pain. I tried to ignore it, but couldn't.

In a way, Virgil was getting back at me. When I'd hit him, my cast had probably broken loose inside. With this new injury within the cast, I wasn't surprised to see blood seeping from the lower end.

I still had Louella's sling around my neck and I placed my arm in it. That helped some, but not enough. The sight of blood dripping though my fingers made me feel weak and light-headed. I pulled up and fumbled in my saddlebag for the canteen. I not only drank from it, I splashed water on my face as well.

I spurred Dublin on again. I had to get back. Oh! How different my earlier ride up this trail had been . . . so beautiful, so idyllic. Now the pain was getting unbearable, I seldom had known such misery. Earlier I'd prayed to be delivered from Virgil's clutches. Now I prayed a pioneer prayer, "Oh God, in this time of need, help me lest I perish!"

The loss of blood was draining my meager strength away.

My arm felt like it was swelling. The pressure and pain sent an urgent message to my brain: Cut the cast off! Get it off!

The sun hadn't set, but a large black cloud came before my eyes. I knew that I was about to pass out.

I pulled up and slid to the ground. Seated on a nearby rock, I began to cut, then frantically stab at the cast with my knife. A piece of it broke away, but the physical exertion sapped my strength. The black cloud took over.

I awoke to the sweet singing of Song Sparrows. Sun streamed gold and green above me in the canopy of pine and cedar. I was chilled through to the bone, and yet my spirit soared at being alive. I sat up and took stock.

The pain in my arm was bearable, and the bleeding had stopped. While unconscious, I'd made a comeback, and I knew my prayers had been answered. I followed up with: "Thank you, God . . . now please stay with me while I end this."

Still light-headed, I looked around for Dublin. Had he trotted back to Virgil? Concerned at not seeing him, I faced the possibility of having to walk to safety. I'd be hard pressed to make it.

Hungry and thirsty, my heart fell. I'd left my saddlebag on Dublin.

The sound of running water cheered me some. At least I could begin the hard hike down the trail with a refreshing drink of water.

Following the sound of a stream, I left the trail and stumbled down through the undergrowth.

Skiddoo! There was Dublin, drinking from the creek.

Dublin could be my salvation. But would he shy away from me?

I gently approached with, "Easy boy, easy . . . eeeeasy . . . and my hand shook as I reached out and grasped his reins.

Trembling with relief and numb with cold, I leaned on

the saddle and hugged the big horse. "Oh Dublin," I sighed. "Thank you for staying with me."

For his part, Dublin nickered his usual welcome and nuzzled me with his wet nose.

He seemed to say, "Well, of course I'm here for you."

After a quick breakfast from Tilly's sack, we were off. Now, more optimistic than ever, my spirit sang as we sped through the forest.

On we traveled until the trail led to a large stream that rushed by, white with froth, as it plunged over its bed of rocks and large stones.

How strange! On the way up I had not been in the mood to notice landmarks, but I certainly would have remembered this whitewater crossing. No! We'd not traveled this way before. Somehow, I'd gotten off on a side trail. The trail led to the riverbank and took up on the other side. The crossing was about fifty feet across. The stream's steep banks offered no other place to cross. Was I heading in the right direction? I pulled up. The sun should be over my right shoulder. It was. I figured we should be traveling downhill. We were.

Wheeling Dublin around, we doubled back, watching for a fork in the trail.

Squirrels scurried about and a cottontail rabbit shot across in front of us. I thrilled to the repeated raucous sound of a Stellers Jay, and the pleasant call of the Song Sparrow. But inner tension tightened my stomach as long stretches of unfamiliar forest slid by.

I refused to admit that I was lost. But why hadn't we intersected the route that led out of here?

I dismounted and sagged down to rest on some fallen pine boughs. How had this happened? I thought back to the last time that I'd been following the right trail.

It had been when I'd awakened this morning.

Yes, and then what?

I'd found Dublin down by the creek.

What had I done then?

I'd used stepping stones to cross the creek to him to the OTHER SIDE.

That might be it!

In my cloudy state of mind, we'd gone up together to a trail, a DIFFERENT trail.

And we had taken off on it. I had to go back, find that spot, cross over, and pick up the original route.

I knelt down and examined the hoof tracks. There were none of our fresh tracks ahead of us. That told me we'd already overshot the spot I was looking for. We turned back and continued on, looking for the place where Dublin's hoof prints came up from the creek.

Within minutes I heard the sound of rushing water. And Skidoo! I spotted hoof marks coming from the underbrush where earlier I'd led Dublin up the wrong side.

Quickly I guided the surefooted horse down, across the creek, and up the other side to the original trail. I'd done it!

What a relief, we were back, heading down to the crossroads.

As we cantered on down I thought, "Sure is easy to get turned around in the woods."

twelve

RETURN TO THE MOUNTAIN

I t was high noon when I saw the Connor farm ahead.

Skidoo! Good to be back! I'd come to love it.

As we headed down the driveway, I fought back tears as a flood of relief ran through me. It had been a wild and dangerous attempt and I'd failed to rescue Jasper . . . but was lucky beyond words to have survived.

I'd ridden out and had been surprised by trouble, had escaped capture, and had encountered wild animals and fought off Virgil.

In spite of my up-beat mood, there remained a worrisome knot in my stomach about Jasper. Did Virgil recover from the blow on the head enough to hike back to his cabin and Jasper? Or was Jasper still penned up, neglected and alone?

I desperately yearned to go to him. But first, I had to get help for my aching arm and build up my strength. I prayed that when I did get back up on the mountain, Jasper would still be there.

Jeb walked out smiling and waving to greet me. In minutes I was once again enjoying the farm family's hospitality. No more sleeping in the barn. This time Ezra moved in to bunk with Fred so I could use his bedroom. I cut my cast off and Tilly brought in a tub and pails of hot water so I could bathe.

When I came back to the kitchen, Louella ran over and gave me a quick hug.

"Casey we were really worried when you turned south to look after your horse."

We settled in at the table as I outlined what had happened.

"Well, I found Jasper, but I also got involved with the polecat that stole him from me." I explained.

Louella frowned. "And you with a broken arm!"

"Well, without the cast on my arm, I wouldn't have made it back out again."

I gave some details of the fight and Louella jumped up and came to me.

"Casey, have you re-injured your arm?" she cried.

She rolled up my sleeve and caught her breath in shock at my completely black and blue arm, now with an ugly gash in it from the cracked cast.

As she put a pan of water on the stove to heat, she cried. "Your arm won't heal if you don't give it chance!"

Louella patiently washed my arm and disinfected it with rubbing alcohol. That felt cool and good, but I almost passed out when she dabbed tincture of iodine directly on the gash below my elbow.

Then, instead of replacing the cast, she simply tied my arm onto a piece of kindling wood as a splint.

"We'll get another cast on when the gash heals and the swelling goes down," she explained and gently helped me into a sling.

I rolled my eyes as she advised, "You should stay quiet now for the next week or two."

"No way!" I said to myself.

Over dinner I detailed my confrontation with Virgil Troaz.

"So Troaz might still be lying up there on the trail, where you clubbed him?" asked Fred.

"Maybe." I answered.

"More likely he got himself back to his cabin." Ezra said.

"I'm concerned about Jasper. I'd like to take off first thing tomorrow morning and go back up there." I announced.

Louella looked dismayed as both Fred and Ezra chimed in. "We'll go with you."

Tilly wiped her hands on a hand towel. "Well!" she exclaimed. "If you're bound and determined to go, I can't stop you. But I don't like it!"

"Someone's got to stay and take care of the farm, or I'd go along too," offered Jeb. "Sorry, Tilly, I understand Casey wantin' to get after that skalawag Troaz. There's unfinished business up on the mountain that can't wait."

As usual, Tilly's fine food revived me. My strength came back as I watched Ezra and Fred loading their rifles, getting out riding boots and making other preparations for the journey up the trail to Virgil Troaz's cabin.

I overheard Fred say, "Ya know, Ezra. We kinda figured there was a hideout up there on the mountain. Now we'll smoke out that rat's nest."

Jeb added, "Yes, then we'll all rest easier."

Louella was the first one to finish the meal, and quickly excused herself from the table. I knew Dublin would soon be receiving her expert attention. But it wasn't until the next morning that I discovered that she had also made her own preparations for the next day.

That night while dozing off, I'd heard Louella and Tilly in serious conversation, speaking in low tones. Then, after a hearty breakfast, I noticed that Louella had saddled up and was set to join us. Ezra and Fred seemed unfazed by this, but I had misgivings. I had disposed of his rifle, but if Virgil had another gun, and if we cornered him on the mountain, he'd probably shoot to kill.

The sun was peeking over the ridge as Dublin and I set the pace on the way to Virgil's cabin.

We soon found ourselves in timber country.

Alert to possible danger, I constantly scanned the area up ahead. We neared the place where I'd spent the night unconscious. I recognized the stream and knew that the other trail lay just beyond it. As I tried to see some trace of that other trail, I caught sight of a huge animal loping along over there. It quickly moved ahead of us.

Skidoo! It was the cat, that friendly cougar!

We stopped to water the horses and I leaned back against a tree to relax my throbbing arm. I'd strolled up away from the creek to a high spot where I could also survey the trail ahead.

No sooner had I made myself comfortable, than I heard a purring sound behind me.

I couldn't believe it! I would never have expected my cougar to find me again, but it had. It came over and nestled against me.

I feared that if any one of the Connors looked up and saw the big cat, they'd whip out a rifle and shoot. I hadn't told them about this unusual animal, and of course they would think me in serious danger.

I thought, "Hey! Maybe I am." But I felt right about going along with my cougar's friendliness to me.

My cougar. Hmm. I decided to give her the name Cleo, because her eyes had the markings I had seen on Egyptian drawings of Cleopatra.

So as Cleo and I sat on the rise, down below the others were speaking in low tones. I knew that they would soon see me with Cleo. Calling to them wouldn't help and might unnerve Cleo. What to do?

I returned Cleo's affection by slowly putting my arm around her. And then I put on my biggest smile and happily gazed down at my three companions. I hoped the peaceful sight of Cleo and me cuddling would forestall a violent reaction.

It did. Ezra was the first to glance my way. He blinked. Then he blinked again and nudged Fred. Fred got a little pale and shook his head at me. Then Louella's red ponytail swung around. She did a double take. All three stared in total amazement.

I could read Louella' expression. She was thinking, "Casey, you stupid city kid! Get away from that mountain lion before you get your head chewed off!"

These had been difficult days for me, but this was fun. I couldn't resist responding to the big cat. It was more than showing off . . . I wouldn't go out of my way for that. But Cleo's being kittenish with me seemed so disarming that I went along with her playfulness.

As the three stood in horror of what would happen to me if the huge wild animal attacked, Cleo turned and licked my ear. I didn't like her rough tongue, but I responded by putting my head on her shoulder and I laughed inside when Ezra slowly sat down on a log to quiet his shaking knees. Fred reverently took off his hat as though in the presence of a miracle, and Louella looked on, expecting the worst.

The horses hadn't gotten wind of the big cat, and the show of affection continued. Still purring, so loudly that I suspected the sound carried down to the onlookers, Cleo slowly rolled over on her back and put her huge paws in the air. As I reached over and stroked her tummy, she loved it . . . stretching and preening. To top things off, as my fingers found an itchy spot, Cleo scratched the air with her back paw, moaning in ecstasy.

But I had a problem. When I stopped petting her, Cleo turned her head and bumped me slightly . . . her way of saying, "Don't stop!"

What to do now? This had been very entertaining, but I needed a way out.

Then inspiration hit. I picked up a large pinecone with my free hand and gently lobbed it over the reclining lion into the ferns beyond.

Skidoo! Cleo's sensitive ears picked up the sound and she sprang up and crouched . . . slowly stalking what might have been a small animal at the spot of the sound.

Thus freed, I rose up, tiptoed down, prepared to stop anyone from pulling out a rifle. I took Dublin's reins and started to mount up.

The others moved toward their horses with the same idea in mind.

Still uneasy, my companions were eager to move out. I intended to ride up the trail as though I'd simply had an encounter with one of God's friendly creatures . . . hardly worth a comment.

But as I put my foot in the stirrup, Virgil Troaz appeared just ahead brandishing a rifle. He shouted, "All of you, stand where you are!"

I was shocked at our bad luck. I knew Virgil couldn't let us go. He was a wanted man and I'd found his hideout.

"Step away from your horses and put your hands up." He commanded.

My mind reeled, I felt helpless to stop what was about to happen. And it was my fault. If only I hadn't gone back to the Connors. I should have contacted a lawman and told him what I knew.

But then, I remembered that it doesn't help to think, "if only," and a second later, I noticed a movement in the underbrush behind Virgil.

My mind flashed to Cleo! She and I had probably been out of sight as the outlaw came up to us. While she investigated the sound in the ferns, she'd been hidden from view. Now she seemed to be stalking Virgil!

"Tether your horses. You first," Virgil said, coolly staring at me.

"Where?' I asked, stalling for time.

"By that birch," he growled, pointing the rifle at me.

I tied Dublin to the tree, prayed for help, and turned, expecting to receive a bullet through my heart.

"This is for trailing me up here and bashing me on the head."

I froze as Virgil's finger began to squeeze the trigger.

But just then, two hundred pounds of mountain lion sprang out of the brush and swept Virgil off his feet. The rifle went flying. Ezra pounced and trussed the outlaw up quick as roping a calf.

Cleo had hit Virgil's shoulder with her forepaws, nimbly flying on across him as he'd gone down.

Now she stood facing back, swishing her tail, ready for action. But when she saw things were well in hand, the huge cat gracefully turned, and disappeared up the slope.

With pounding heart, I stepped back to Dublin and took his reins. The other three horses were gone . . . spooked when the Cougar had charged. Dublin, wise and steady, had whinnied and stamped his hooves with excitement, but he hadn't pulled his tether.

Then I heard Louella calling to her horse that was fast disappearing down the trail.

I jumped on Dublin shouting, "Hop on!" Louella mounted

in front of me. Her ponytail pleasantly smacked me in the face as I passed the reins to her. Now we had a rider with two good arms to chase down the horses.

Dublin didn't need urging to take up the chase. As we sped down the trail, I had to squeeze Louella's waist with my good arm to keep from bouncing off. Still, it took another half mile to run down Louella's blowing and snorting mare, Merelda, and rein her in.

Farther down yet, the other two horses were wildly heading for home. In seconds, Louella switched to her own horse. Merelda reared up as the able cowgirl shouted, "Follow me!" and sped off in hot pursuit.

Farther on I watched Louella bring another horse to a stop. Without a word between us, I galloped up, took the reins of Fred's horse, hitching them around my saddle's pommel.

With one lame arm I didn't feel up to leading an excited horse back up the trail, so I just sat and waited. Sure enough, some ten minutes later, Louella's skillful riding paid off again. I spotted her leading Ezra's horse back to us.

Louella and I rode along in silence to where Ezra and Fred were holding Virgil captive.

What was she thinking? Did she blame me for this near-tragic episode? She could be furious at me for starting the whole thing by foolishly playing around with a potentially vicious cougar.

The four of us had set out to capture a desperate outlaw. I'd lost my focus and had almost brought disaster down on us.

However, thinking back to what had happened, I felt little remorse. I'd been just as surprised as anyone that Cleo had come to me in a playful mood. Any sudden act on my part to stop the playfulness could have triggered the animal's wild instinct with serious results.

As it had been earlier, when Louella had blamed me for

mistreating Dublin, there'd been no point in my trying to explain. I didn't offer an excuse now either. After all, I could have tossed the diversion pinecone earlier than I had.

As we rode in, Ezra and Fred joyfully hailed us. "Hey! You ran them down! The way they took off, they coulda been in Boise by now," shouted Fred.

I quickly responded, "Yeah, they'd be running yet, except for Louella."

Ezra smiled at his sister as he took possession of his horse. "Way to go Lou! Thanks. We're one horse short as it is."

The nice words didn't seem to have any calming effect on Louella. She dismounted and turned to me with eyes blazing and fists ready to strike. I didn't think she'd hit me with my arm in a sling, but just in case, I stood ready to duck.

"Louella! I said quickly, "While Ezra and Fred are taking Virgil back, would you come with me to search for Jasper? We'll need to ride double again, and if we find him, I'll be glad for the company back down the trail."

Fred jumped in with, "That's a good plan, Lou. Casey's horse could be tethered just up the trail where this bushwhacker left him."

Without a word, Louella moved to Dublin and mounted up, waiting for me to get on behind. Seconds later, she'd spurred Dublin to a loping canter and we quickly hit the trail in search of Jasper. I assumed that Virgil who was sitting with a scowl on his face under a fir tree, would ride Merelda back.

thirteen

THE VIRGIL TROAZ HIDE-OUT

*L*ouella remained silent as we rode through patches of brilliant sunshine.

Along the way we flushed a covey of quail, a jay chattered and we awakened a roly-poly badger who made an ugly face at us and scurried away.

Aware of Louella's silent anger, I still managed to live for the moment . . . matching Dublin's smooth motion, I thought, "What a joy this is . . . cantering along on this perfect autumn day, with a fine young woman for a companion."

We hadn't gone far when Louella pulled up and cried out, "Casey, look up there! Is that your horse?"

In a cluster of fern and scrub oak I caught sight of my fine horse. There, peacefully cropping bunchgrass stood Jasper.

I slid down and ran to him. Finally, after so many worrisome days, I could once again know the thrill of putting my arm around his neck and greeting him.

"Oh Jasper! At last, I have you back."

As he gave me his usual throaty greeting, I loved the welcoming look in his eyes, the feel of his fine coat, and the smell of him. What a joy to have him back!

I spoke softly. "Have you been cared for, Boy? Are you all right?"

As Jasper swished his tail and gave me his low whinny, he moved his head up and down as though nodding, yes.

Before I mounted up, Louella and I checked under his cinch and saddle. All seemed to be O.K.

I turned to Louella who sat smiling at me. "Well, Lou, what do you think? It's still early in the day. Are you up to riding on to Virgil's cabin to check it out?"

Louella sat for a few seconds then asked, "Why?"

I was curious about the cabin in the woods. Actually I hoped to find and return the "stash" that the deputy said Virgil had stolen from the old settler. I needed to give a good answer.

"Why don't we give ourselves an hour to look things over up there, then we'll have more details to give the sheriff when we make our report."

"Well, Casey, that's good thinking," said Louella pleasantly. "But we'll have to head back before too long if we want to get home by sundown."

Now my heart was really singing. I had Jasper under me again and I loved the spirited way that he took to the trail. Then, too, Louella seemed to be getting over her temper snit.

Arriving at the Troaz hideout with the sun showing midday, we pushed through the unlocked door.

The sparsely furnished one-room cabin was a shambles. A bare bunk stood against the far wall opposite a native-stone fireplace. It looked to be the source of heat and the place where Virgil cooked his meals. An iron pot hanging on a hinged bar could be swung in over the coals, and a coffeepot, blackened with use, stood on the hearth.

A simple table built out from the wall had one crude chair under it. A few articles of clothing were scattered around and some wooden crates, all empty, littered the floor.

"Lou, I don't see any food around. Doesn't appear that Virgil was planning to stay here. I think we might have captured him on his way out."

Louella seemed to agree. "Probably . . . and if that's the case, we won't find anything more in the shed than we have here."

A quick search of the shed turned up nothing of any value.

Then the thrill of an idea hit me.

"Lou!" I shouted, "If Virgil was clearing out . . . on the run when we stopped him, THAT MEANS HE HAD HIS VALUABLES WITH HIM!"

"Louella's eyes opened wide and together we yelled -- "JASPER'S SADDLEBAG!"

We rushed out to Jasper with Virgil's saddlebag tied on behind. I raised the flap and Louella's hand trembled as she brought out three large leather packets.

"Casey! This is Virgil Troaz's stash! We found it!"

"SKIDOO! Let's have a look!"

We quickly found a grassy area and placed the pouches between us. In the first one we found over a hundred greenbacks in five, ten and twenty dollar denominations.

Louella yelled, "WHOOEE! What a wad of cash!

After a quick count, I exclaimed, "THERE'S OVER TWO THOUSAND DOLLARS HERE."

"Looks like it could be from a bank robbery."

"You could be right, Lou, or ill-gotten gains from gambling. Honest folks don't have this much cash around."

The second packet was heavy with gold coins.

Louella ran her fingers through them. "Casey, I've never seen so much gold in all my life!"

"Nor have I. This might be the old settler's life savings.'"

"Now what do you suppose we'll find in this third pouch?" I asked.

Louella picked it up. "Feels like it could be more paper money." She released its strap and pulled out three legal papers. The first was a deed to a saloon on the Seattle waterfront. The second gave clear title to ten acres of timberland near Tacoma and to my amazement, the third conferred ownership of a fishing boat. Then, rubbing my eyes to be sure, I re-read the name of the boat. It was the SILVER BELLE!

"Lou!" I cried in excitement. "I know that boat! I was actually shanghaied to Alaska on it! Virgil must have won these properties in high stakes poker games."

Louella sat in open-mouthed wonder as I picked up the legal title for the SILVER BELLE. On the line that read: FORMER OWNER was the scrawled signature of Captain Bin Dunn. The NEW OWNER line had been left blank.

Louella's eyes became wide with wonder as I briefly told of my fishing boat adventure to Alaska. I told of Red Snapper and how he and his crew often went to The Anchor saloon on Seattle's waterfront while they were in port.

It didn't surprise me that the captain had played poker and lost, but to put up his fishing boat as a bet? Amazing!

When I finished, she said, "Casey, I didn't know you'd been involved in such a harrowing experience."

I sat back and smiled at her. "Well, it hasn't been a slack time here lately either."

My dry comment relieved the tension between us . . . she burst out laughing. Now that I had Jasper back, I laughed until my shoulder ached.

"Oh Casey!" Louella said putting her hand on mine. "I'm sorry for giving you a bad time. I know I have a temper. But you've got to explain how you charmed that big cat. At times you can be so exasperating!"

"Lou, I haven't a clue as to why that cougar is so friendly with me. While hiding from Virgil yesterday the big cat just came over, lay down along side of me and took a nap. I can't explain it."

"It took a nap?"

"Yes, and I was so exhausted, that when it began to snore, I fell asleep with it."

"Snore?"

At that, Louella rolled her eyes and flopped back on the grass. She lay there shaking her head from side to side for a few seconds before jumping to her feet.

"Casey, I can't stand to hear any more right now. Let's get back to our quiet little farm before anything else happens out here."

fourteen

MAN OF THE WOODS

After a downhill gallop, we came to the place where I'd found Dublin drinking from the stream. I knew that if we crossed over to the opposite side, and rode on up the other trail, we'd come to a river and the whitewater crossing.

Deciding not to mention the woodsy pathway on the far side, I nevertheless suggested that we stop to water the horses.

I looked this way and that for Cleo and was relieved that I didn't spot her.

Just as I mounted up for the last leg back to the Connor farm, Jasper whinnied and stamped his hooves. I sensed something unusual.

"Lou, let's hold up. Jasper's acting strangely."

Then we both heard a loud moaning sound from across the creek.

I called out "I'm going to check it out," as Jasper and I once again crossed over to the trail on the other side.

Then I caught sight of something so astonishing that for several seconds I simply stopped and stared.

Just ahead lay a narrow cart with an old man pinned under

it. One of the four wheels lay on the ground with part of a broken axle attached to it. I assumed that the man had been loading limestone when the axle snapped, pinning his shin to the ground.

I jumped off and noticed the wagon was painted green with rose colored floral designs.

Kneeling down, I observed the man's craggy, handsome face and long, dark, hair streaked with gray. He seemed of large build, lean and strong. A brown felt hat set off with a heron feather lay beside him.

His eyes fluttered open. "Oh my goodness," he said and touched the back of his head.

"Well, hello young man. I hit my head when the wagon fell on me. Thank the Good Lord you've come. Trieste and I could have died out here."

"I'll find a tree limb and pry the wagon off of you." I said quickly.

Then I noticed Trieste, an animal harnessed to the wagon. How strange! Trieste had the appearance of a short-horned elk.

As I searched for a limb, it almost seemed that the man and his quaint wagon pulled by a wild animal, were all part of a child's folktale and I was somehow being drawn into it.

Inside the wagon were several large slabs of pink limestone that had been cut from the nearby hillside. I lightened the load by lifting out three of the slabs, then, having stacked them on the trail beside the broken axle; I began to use them as a fulcrum and the tree limb as a lever to raise the wagon, just as Louella rode up on Dublin.

The man looked up at her and said, "Hello, young lady. You are just in time to pull me out when your friend here frees my leg."

In a flash, Louella dropped down on her knees and seconds

later slid him out.

"Now," she said. "Let's check out your leg, Mr. Man O'Woods."

"My name is Anton Hoffman," the man said, and despite the injured leg, he smiled. "But you are right. I am a man of the woods."

"Hello, Mr. Hoffman, I'm Louella."

Totally in charge now with her healing instincts taking over, the would-be nurse gently rolled up the pant leg of the injured shin.

"Hmmm, looks like you're lucky Mr. Woodsman, the bone might be cracked, but probably not broken. You'll need to get around on a crutch for a few weeks."

"Well, first I'll need to get back to my home. If you would be so good as to unharness Trieste, I'll try to ride her back to where I live.

My mind awhirl with the thought of riding an elk, I broke in. "My name is Casey, Mr. Hoffman. How far do you live from here?"

"Oh, Casey. Except for his accident, Trieste and I would have returned to our home well before sunset."

"Have you ridden your elk before?"

"Yes, for short distances, she's strong and still in her prime. If you help me up on her, I'm sure we'll make it back."

"Excuse me, Sir, but I traveled this trail once before to where it crosses another stream that runs strong and fresh. Would you be going that way?"

At the mention of the whitewater crossing, Mr. Hoffman seemed impressed. "Yes, and I know a favorable crossing of those rapids."

While we spoke, Louella had brought out a first aid kit and had cleansed the bruised and swollen shin, then she wrapped it loosely with a gauze bandage for protection.

After checking the back of Mr. Hoffman's head, she re-marked, "Lucky again, just a bump. Then staring at Trieste with a raised eyebrow, she spoke up.

"Mr. Hoffman, I feel strongly that without a saddle, you might have another accident on the way back to your home. I don't feel right about leaving you to fend for yourself on the trail.

I agreed with Louella's sensible approach.

"That's my thought too, Mr. Hoffman. I'd have no peace of mind without knowing that you made it back to your home safely." I said firmly.

"But," the injured man said sorrowfully, "I can't ask you to take me all the way to where I live."

"All right!" I said. "Then accept the loan of one of our horses. One is mine, and I have the 'say so' about the other one."

Then Mr. Hoffman surprised us. "I know that big chestnut horse. I recognized it when you rode in, young lady."

Shocked by this, we waited for an explanation.

"You see," Mr. Hoffman went on. "He belongs to the out-law. Now that you and your companions have captured the man who threatened you, I understand why you are caring for his horse."

"B-but," I stammered. "How do you know all this?"

"I was watching from a thicket when the outlaw was about to shoot. I gave my Catsala the signal to attack him . . . just in time, I think."

"Your Cat-sa-la?"

"Yes, the mountain lion who helped you, I raised her from a kitten when hunters killed her mother."

At that, Louella put her hand on her forehead and said, "You TAMED a cougar?"

"Yes. Trisete here is proof that I have a way with animals.

She pulls my cart, but she can go free anytime she wants."

I looked at Louella. "Lou, I think that we need to entrust Dublin to Mr. Hoffman. Somehow, we'll straighten everything out later on . . . after my arm heals."

Louella looked relieved. The plan would allow us to get back to the Connor's farm without delay.

"Yes," she said. "Mr. Hoffman, what do you say to riding Dublin? He's a fine horse and will see you home safely."

"I accept your kind offer. I will take Dublin, as you call him, and treat him kindly until spring when I will return him to you."

Louella transferred her bag of belongings to Jasper's saddlebag that contained Virgil's three packets. Mr. Hoffman mounted up with his good left leg carrying his weight.

We unharnessed Trieste who had been waiting patiently. I'd never seen an elk up close. Out of curiosity, I put my hand on her smooth back. She paid no attention to me.

Before he rode off, the man of the woods spoke seriously. "Thank you Louella and Casey, I have the gift of reading hearts. Yours are pure. You will be blessed for your kindness."

He pointed at the limestone slabs. "Place these pieces of stone over there underneath that big cedar tree. Hide them amongst the fern.

"The tenth of April marks a special day in my life. On that date many years ago, my young bride and I headed west to settle in Oregon. On April 10th this spring, I hope both of you will return to this spot.

"A map will be hidden in the midst of the limestone that will guide you to my home. Please don't tell others about this. If you come to me, I'll not only return Dublin, I will have an unusual gift for each of you. Rest assured I will not be outdone by the kindness you showed me today."

Then, with a nod, the man of the woods guided Dublin

down the narrow pathway. With Trieste gracefully following behind, they disappeared in sunlit mist.

Louella and I stood staring, as in a trance. Then I looked at the broken wagon . . . just to verify that this little episode had truly taken place.

Louella too stared at it as I lifted the three pink slabs, carrying them to the secure spot by the cedar and rolled the wheel with the broken axle off the main path.

Then, without a word, Louella mounted up and, with her arms around my waist, we again shared one horse as Jasper happily cantered through the warmth of a fall afternoon . . . the three of us gliding through the most beautiful and fragrant forest on God's earth.

The farther we rode, the more dreamlike became the time spent with the man of the woods and his four-footed friend.

Mr. Lambrusco's inspirational words came to mind. "A few fortunate people will have at least one highly spiritual encounter in their lifetimes. How will you know when it happens? Ah! You will know because of its transcendence!"

Here in the woods, it had happened. I'd been elevated to a higher level of being. More fully alive, my spirit rode the crest of a wave.

We turned northwest at the crossroads with my joyful thought, "soon I'll enjoy the warmth of the Connor family's home and hearth."

Hearth . . . a word like heart . . . rich with meaning for me. As hearth is the center of a home, I realized heart means the center of me, where I live. And I thrilled to Mr. Hoffman's words. He'd looked into our hearts and had seen "that they were pure." Skidoo!

fifteen

THE REWARD

When Louella and I rode in to the Connor farm, Ezra and Fred had returned to the ranch after turning Virgil over to the sheriff.

While feasting on a special meal Tilly Connor had prepared to celebrate our return, Ezra and Fred described how surprised and gratified the sheriff of Umatilla County had been to take custody of Virgil Troaz.

As we enjoyed the juicy roast beef and creamy mashed potatoes, Louella and I noticed how bright-eyed and jovial the brothers were, and for that matter, Tilly and Jeb were in a happy mood too, ready to laugh at the slightest bit of humor.

Finally, I put down my fork. "All right now. What's going on?" I asked.

Louella and I glanced at each other with heightened curiosity, when Fred said, "You tell 'em Ezra."

"Well," Ezra began. "Turns out that we earned a $2500 reward for bringin' Virgil in."

Louella jumped up. "Twenty five hundred dollars!" She hopped around and clapped her hands. "That's just what we need right now! We can pay cash for high quality seed corn.

Then we can grind what we have saved back for seed, and sell it as cornmeal."

Jeb Connor sat back chuckling. "Yes, Louella, we had that same idea." He went on. "But we feel that a chunk of the reward should go to Casey, our young helpful friend, here."

Touched by the Connor's kindness, I quickly responded.

"The reward is great news, but I wasn't any help capturing Virgil. In fact, I let down my guard up there. I wouldn't feel right about taking any part of a reward. But thank you for the generous thought."

From the corner of my eye, I caught Louella's look of admiration. I went on before anyone had a chance to comment. "Now, Louella and I have a surprise too."

Louella quickly produced Virgil's saddle bag. We showed the amazed Connors the contents of the three bags.

Tilly said it for us all. "Good heavens! Seein' all this stolen gold and money taken in gambling, just makes me feel sick inside."

The next several minutes we talked over the possibilities of just how Virgil's loot would be legally disposed of.

Pleased that the old settler back in Washington would undoubtedly have his stolen coins restored to him, we decided that I would transport the saddlebag to the sheriff in Pendleton where Virgil was being held.

After a good night's sleep and a fine breakfast, I said my good-byes to Jeb, Tilly, Fred and Ezra, and headed for the barn with Louella.

Tracking down Jasper with my broken arm had seemed almost hopeless. But with the strong support of the Connors, I had Jasper back and we'd captured the thief who'd stolen him from me.

I felt a tingle of excitement at the thought of turning over Virgil's loot to the sheriff on my way back to K2.

It was time to express my gratitude. "Louella, you folks have welcomed me like a member of your family."

While saddling up Jasper, she said, "Well, Casey, so far as I'm concerned, you are a true family member." And then she came over and gently put her arms around me and kissed me lightly on the cheek. "I'm not ashamed to say that I've come to love you like a brother."

"Skidoo! Thanks for that, Lou." I said, blushing and wishing I had two good arms. "Now more than ever, I'm sorry to leave."

In her sensible way, Louella said, "But you have to see to your arm, return to your folks and maybe help that poor settler get his stolen property back."

"Yes. But in about four months do you and I have a date? I'd like to meet Anton Hoffman again and see about Dublin."

"Yes, Casey. We have a date for the tenth of April to see where the mountain man lives. If that's during your Spring Vacation, maybe you could arrive here ahead of time. We could have a nice visit, and on the tenth, we'll ride up to that whitewater crossing together."

I mounted up. "Well, that's something to look forward to. Along about the first of April, it'll take more than a broken arm to keep me away from here."

Louella beamed, then said, "So long, Casey," and, as she turned to go, I just couldn't resist. I reached down and gave a little tug on her ponytail.

With eyes blazing, Louella swung around. "Hey you!" she protested.

I galloped off, shouting, "Thanks for caring for me, nurse!"

sixteen

HEADING HOME

*T*he sheriff of Umatilla County was more than pleased to receive Virgil's valuables.

While I waited, he phoned T. J. Torgeson at the Benton County seat in Prosser, Washington. From the description, the deputy identified the packet of coins as that belonging to a Mr. Jesse Crisp and his wife, the settlers who'd been robbed by Virgil Troaz.

T J asked to talk to me.

"That you, Casey Jones?" he asked.

"Yes, I'm on my way back to the K2 Ranch near Arborville."

"I heard you tracked down the bushwhacker, Troaz, despite that busted arm. Mighty impressive."

"Well, I helped some, the Connor brothers did the work of bringing him in."

"You got your hoss back, too, eh."

"Yes sir, I'm back on Jasper."

"An' now you jus' turned in Virgil's loot to the sheriff. I need to talk to ya 'bout that packet of coins. I convinced the sheriff there it belongs to our man an' his wife that was bushwhacked.

DUBLIN

ANNIE

CASEY

The sheriff sez he'll count it, then let you sign fer it so's you can bring it up here to be returned to its rightful owners. Do you feel up to that?"

"Yes. Could you come to the Kinsman home in Arborville?"

"Good place to meet. I've heard of Harry Kinsman. This way, maybe I'll get a chance to meet him."

"O.K. TJ, I plan to head home early tomorrow morning."

The sheriff got me to the local doctor who put my arm in a cast, treated me to a restaurant meal and let me bed down in a courthouse anteroom. After a fair night's sleep and an early breakfast in the jail's kitchen, I was on my way before sunrise.

Jasper'd had good care at the stable behind the jail. He was full of spirit and pranced up the road leading to the Columbia River Gorge. I soon set him to a lively canter until we reached the ferry landing. By noon we'd crossed over, heading up and over the bluff.

My arm began to ache, but I ignored it as we moved back across the pristine grasslands Horse Heaven Hills. I thought, "Some cowboy should sing a song about this wide expanse of green . . . this lush, elevated plain."

In daylight now, my eyes drank in the sight. The tall grass riffling in the breeze resembled ocean waves and reminded me of my voyage aboard the SILVER BELLE.

With the breeze full in my face, I breathed deeply of the chill air. Like a cool drink of well water, it was so stimulating that my spirits soared.

Then as we rollicked through the tall grass, a thrill shot through me as a herd of wild horses, manes and tails flying, streamed by, running free as the wind.

Skidoo! What a beautiful sight!

Jasper seemed to be happy to be back. He picked up the pace as we rounded the curved road into K2 and I said a prayer of thanks that the settlers' coins would be returned to them, and that Jasper and I were home at last.

seventeen

WELCOME HOME

*T*hat evening, when I'd entered the paddock, two of the K2 hands, Sut Fritipan and Chin Lee had come out to meet me.

Chin Lee immediately took charge of Jasper, yelling, "Hi there, Casey. Welcome back!"

Sut drawled, "Well, dude, ya kinda took yer ol' sweet time a getting' back here; 'cept fer that busted arm, I'd guess ya'd dallied along the way with some cute filly of a gal."

"Ha! Is that why you're so late getting back?" joked Chin Lee.

Blushing at how near Sut had come to the truth, I protested, "Hey you guys, a horse thief knocked me off Jasper and put me through a powerful lot of misery before I got him back."

"Well, from the looks of things," Sut drawled, "Jasper got through it in better shape than you did."

I left the fellas chuckling to themselves as I carried my saddlebag with the precious packet to the K2 ranch house.

Not just tired, but bone weary, I shuffled through the back door. I loved the warmth of the kitchen with its homey smells.

My heart swelled with happiness.

Bernie and Stella Wellman, the K2 caretakers, were happy to see me. Bernie exclaimed, "Well! Look who's wandered in! What happened? You and Jasper take a wrong turn somewheres?"

Too exhausted for small talk, I nonetheless forced a half smile and made the effort to be cheerful.

"You could say that, Bernie. I sure did get off on a different trail, an Oregon trail."

Kind Stella rushed over and took my hand. "Welcome back, Casey!" Then, with typical concern, she looked me over. "My, you look so gaunt . . . and with an arm in a cast, too. Looks like you need a hot meal and a good night's sleep."

"Sounds great. I'll start with a shower and be right back for some supper."

Stella took time out from baking an apple pie to serve me a big bowl of her delicious stew. My friend Cal Paluskin came by and joined Bernie and me at the table.

When, during the telling of my adventure, I mentioned Virgil Troaz, he put down his coffee cup, eyes blazing.

"Troaz? That man is bad medicine! Going against him . . . very dangerous."

"Well, early on, I was just fired up to get Jasper back from him."

"Uhunh." Cal grunted. "Didn't the deputy sheriff warn you about him?"

"Not at first. He just referred to him as a 'bushwhacker.' What have you heard?"

"He will kill a man for no reason, cheats at cards, and some say he has a hideout way up in the mountains."

"His hideout?" I paused with a chunk of homemade bread half way to my mouth. "Yes, that's where I found Jasper."

Bernie's mouth dropped open.

After a few seconds of stunned silence, Stella, about to refill our cups, instead put the coffee pot back on the stove with a bang and exclaimed, "Merciful heavens! You went up to that outlaw's place . . . alone?"

"Well, yes. Troaz had knocked me off Jasper by the Columbia. That's how I got this broken arm. The Deputy was hot on his trail, and Troaz needed a fresh horse.

He took Jasper. A few days later, riding the big chestnut Troaz'd left me, I tracked him to his place in the woods."

Cal raised his hand with a question in his eyes. "Wait! You tracked Troaz? How?"

"Actually I tracked Jasper's tracks. Bernie, remember the three diamond horseshoe we used to re-shoe Jasper?"

"Yeah. Pretty dang clever of you to remember that."

Stella joined us at the table, wide-eyed with disbelief. "You tellin' us you rode all the way down into Oregon with a broken arm and took on a desperate outlaw?"

"It sounds worse than it was." I said, trying to temper the facts. "I'd stayed over with some kindly farm folks and got a cast on my arm."

Bernie, took a piece of bread to go with his coffee. As he picked up a butter knife, he observed, "sounds like you're tryin' to butter up the truth. Fact is, you went in where even seasoned lawmen wouda been a mite trepadatious."

"After what happened next, I have to admit it was foolish." I added.

No one said a word, so I went on. "Well, soon as I rode up, Troaz got the drop on me, tied me up and left me out in a shed.

"Cal, I used the knife you'd given me to cut myself free, then high-tailed it down the trail. But Troaz caught up with me and we tussled."

Bernie repeated the word in total amazement, "Tussled! You mean you fought him hand to hand . . . with one good arm?"

By this time, feeling very self-conscious, trail weary, and somewhat ashamed, I just wanted to get this storytelling ordeal over with. I must have been red-faced and a bit desperate.

"Yes, but we both had knives."

At the mention of knives, Stella jumped up from the table. "Land sakes!" she cried. "How in the world did you survive?"

"I knocked him out with my cast."

At that, Cal's brown eyes glowed with a fierce regard for me, but Bernie and Stella seemed stunned and speechless. I left them there and quietly went to my room.

My comfortable bed, like a wonderful magic carpet, wafted me away to the best night's sleep I'd had in over a week. It was mid-morning when I rubbed my eyes, remembering that it was Saturday and my first day back.

Annie, youngest of the Kinsman girls, lingered over breakfast with me. She'd caught an early wagon ride out with Cal Paluskin who'd reported in to my Uncle Harry. Her older sisters, Colette and Neva were still back at Overton Manor, the family's town house.

Annie seemed older than her fifteen years, and was a plainly attractive young lady. When I came down to breakfast she'd been waiting for me. I'd never received such a welcome. She hugged me tight with a rapid-fire explosion of endearing words.

With her cheek next to mine she finally said, "Oh Casey, thank God you're back!" Ignoring my cast, she just hung on tight for another minute.

When she let go, she stood close, blinking back tears. "Casey, I don't know what I'd have done if that outlaw'd killed you."

I took Annie's shaking hand. "Well, I guess you've heard of my close call on the trail. But, Hey! I'm back and except for this bunged up arm, I'm fine!"

Annie managed a smile and sat at the table.

During breakfast, I kept the conversation light, asking about the K2 dog, Lobo, and details of the Overton Manor thanksgiving dinner. But in the back of my mind, I had a thought or two about how different Annie was from Louella. Both girls loved farm life, but despite Annie's aggressive greeting, she had a more gentle nature than Louella.

As I sat looking at Annie, I let my true feelings flow. I was happy to be back. I had become deeply intertwined with everything here.

I'd missed this ranch, with its fields of alfalfa and barley, its hundreds of beef cattle and especially riding up into its vast, forested area to the north, filled with wild things.

And now, after a time away, I saw everything in a new light. My relatives and friends had become very dear to me and I greatly loved them.

I took another sip of coffee. "Annie, I'm glad to be back. I missed you . . . and everyone here. When will I get to see Colette and Neva?"

The timing of that comment couldn't have been better. Annie broke into a radiant smile as she looked over my shoulder. Sixteen year old Colette came up from up behind me followed closely by her older sister, Neva.

What followed was another couple of affectionate greetings from these two vivacious Kinsman girls. But I noticed that their greetings were much more light-hearted than Annie's had been. Possibly, the two older girls had not heard of my close call with the outlaw.

The two joined us at the table and Neva began. "Now, Casey, we want to hear about your adventures. The telegrams we got were skimpy on details."

"Yes, in a nutshell, I was riding back after making a deal

for wool, when a bushwhacker named Troaz attacked me and broke my arm. He stole Jasper. I was able to follow on the horse the outlaw left behind, and some good folks down in Oregon helped me get Jasper back again."

Colette, with her usual flashing eyes asked, "Who took care of your broken arm?"

"A member of a farm family, in Oregon, Lou Connor."

"Well, I'd like to hear more about how you got Jasper back from the outlaw, but maybe that can wait until this evening when you come for dinner," Neva suggested, pushing a curl of dark hair aside. "I expect you'll be coming in to Overton Manor won't you? Your mom and everyone there are really eager to see you."

"Yes, of course, I'll ride Jasper in later this afternoon."

I'd forgotten just how pert and pretty all three Kinsman girls were and I remembered that they still were under the mistaken impression that I was a first cousin of theirs. Somehow, I had to find a way to let them know the truth.

That evening at dinner I enjoyed the attention of all at the table. Uncle Harry with his heavy crop of dark hair and thick mustache, and Aunt Louise with her long blond braids wound on top of her head, were full of questions. My mom sat quietly listening since I'd greeted her earlier and had filled her in on much of my adventure.

Also at the table was Olga Boltus, Aunt Louise's live-in sister. Since the death of her son, Vernon, Aunt Olga had become my friend and mentor of sorts.

As I noticed her at the end of the table, listening intently to me with a kind smile, I marveled at her warm feelings for me. A few months ago, Vernon had tried to kill me. He'd been jealous of my finding favor with Uncle Harry who had dismissed him for incompetence. Back then, it seemed unthinkable that Olga Boltus would warm up to me.

After dinner when we sang a few songs with Neva at the piano, I wondered when I'd be able to get back to playing the guitar . . . maybe in time for Christmas carols.

I stayed over in the nice Overton Manor bedroom reserved for me. After a fine breakfast, I began to catch up on my energy . . . just enjoying the morning's sun streaming through the living room windows when Olga Boltus joined me.

"Casey," she began. "You look a bit frayed around the edges."

"Well, Aunt Olga. I'm tired from all the riding."

"I understand. I shouldn't wonder that there were some difficulties down there in Oregon in addition to those you mentioned."

Olga's comment triggered the telling of how Dr. Lear Bennett had rescued me, my tracking the outlaw with deputy TJ Torgeson, and something of the Connors . . . which was more than I'd had a chance to mention so far, even to my mother.

When I came to Louella's help with my arm, I found myself mentioning than I had chatted with her briefly about my three interesting cousins who aren't really my cousins.

That led to the problem.

"Aunt Olga, please help me. I simply want the fact to come out that, as a girl, my mother was adopted. I want everyone to know the truth."

"Well, of course." Aunt Olga said reassuringly. "It's only right that this bit of Kinsman family history should be brought up to date."

"But How? Mom thinks that my bringing it up wouldn't be quite proper."

"Well, Casey, I must agree with your mother. It would be awkward for either of you to bring it up . . . just out of the blue."

"Well, I can understand that. Those hearing such a comment, would wonder why."

"Exactly. However, I have a way to approach this issue." Olga said calmly.

"Really?" I said with less emotion than I felt.

"Why yes, I am in an ideal position, as a member of the family once removed, to make this announcement so to speak. I shall begin with the fact that Casey Jones through his talent and courage has added luster to the family name. I will conclude with, 'both he and his mother are highly regarded members of the Kinsman family, though by adoption.' "

I just nodded as Olga went on. " 'And this fact, known to the older members of the family, is also known to Casey himself . . . however he, quite modestly, doesn't make a point of it.' "

"But, Aunt Olga, since Uncle Harry and Aunt Louise already know that I'm their nephew by adoption, just how do you plan to announce this?"

"Why, I shall do so quite casually at a gathering of the Arborville Bridge Club. We're scheduled to meet this Tuesday afternoon."

I was a little let down. Telling a piece of family history at a card game? "Gee, Aunt Olga, do you really think that the truth about Mom and me will get around after that?"

Never before had I seen Aunt Olga so consumed with merriment as her soft lyrical laugh filled the room. She took a 'kerchief from her sleeve and dabbed her eyes.

"Oh, Casey, you know that news can be spread by telegraph, and telephone?"

"Yes, of course."

"Well, I would add another . . . tell a bridge club."

"Skidoo! You'll spread word for me by planting a seed of gossip?"

"Exactly. Give it a week or two and the Kinsman family facts will be all over town."

"Aunt Olga! How clever of you."

"Not at all, Casey. Older people simply know more of the ways of the world. You see, another thing in your favor is that some of the members of my bridge club undoubtedly will remember when your mother first came to Overton Manor as a child, and they'll boast about remembering it."

"I see."

"I would think Casey, that you are pleased to be a highly regarded member of the family . . . content with your status as a Kinsman by adoption . . . a position to be proud of but never to brag about."

"Exactly! That's it! Aunt Olga, how can I thank you."

"Casey, perhaps you might wait with your thanks until you see the reaction you receive to this news."

"Reaction?" Truthfully, I hadn't thought that far ahead.

eighteen

TJ TORGESON'S PLAN

After dinner, Uncle Harry and I found ourselves in the Overton Manor library, a wood paneled room filled with hundreds of books, large comfortable chairs and soft carpet. We settled in for a chat as sunlight flooded the room from French windows that opened out to a flower garden.

Ah! Peace and contentment.

For the first time in twelve days, I could favor my sore arm and shoulder and an inner voice said, "There's no place on earth I'd rather be right now."

"Well, Casey," Uncle Harry began with a slight frown. "I truly had second thoughts about sending you down to meet with Rightfoot. I knew you could handle the business part of the trip, but riding alone on the trail can be dangerous."

"So I found out." I replied dryly.

"Yes, from what I've heard, you are lucky to be alive." And with that, Uncle Harry jumped up and used his finger to trace a line across the titles of several leather-bound books on the shelf just behind his desk.

"Aha!" he exclaimed. "Here it is, my book of quotations."

While my uncle scanned the pages I watched with curiosity.

When we had first met at the train station, he'd been so forceful . . . taking me by the arm and insisting that I go with him instead of continuing on to meet with another aunt and uncle in Seattle. That had been a shock, especially since it had been so soon after my father's death.

But now I felt so at home in this big house of his, and I'd not only come to trust and admire him, I actually loved this fine man. I learned too, that Harry Kinsman was respected and admired by all.

Just then he looked up with a smile. "Casey, here's a quotation by Alexander Pope: 'Fools rush in where angels fear to tread.' I was reminded of it as you described your encounter with Virgil Troaz."

I put my head back and sighed. "Well, I've not heard that quote before . . . but must admit it describes what I did up in the Oregon mountains. It was foolish of me."

"Extremely so!"

Uncle Harry began to give me stern advice. I recognized this as another exercise in humility and was truly relieved when Aunt Louise came in to announce that we had a visitor.

"Harry, a deputy sheriff by the name of T. J. Torgeson is here to see you."

I jumped up. "Deputy Torgeson is here to receive the stolen property I brought up from Oregon."

"Oh, I see. Louise, my dear, please show Deputy Torgeson in."

I blurted out, "Sorry, Uncle Harry, I meant to tell you more about it when I gave you that leather packet for safe keeping. But then we went right in to dinner."

"I see. That packet felt like it had coins in it."

"It does. Quite a lot of gold coins."

Uncle Harry raised his eyebrows. "Gold?"

Before I had time to say more, the man I knew as T J strode in and extended his hand to my uncle.

"Ah, good afternoon, suh."

Uncle Harry stood up. "I am Harry Kinsman."

The lawman bore only slight resemblance to the rumpled, dusty T.J. Torgeson who'd handcuffed me at our first meeting.

Now the deputy wore a spotless, dark green uniform with polished brass buttons. He stood with dignity, handsomely erect, his heavy jet-black hair combed straight back, his long mustache groomed to waxed points that curled upwards in a perpetual second smile. He wore no spurs and his fine, black leather boots gleamed without a speck of trail dust. I decided that Deputy Torgeson had driven in by car.

He spoke with confidence. "It is surely a pleasure to meet you, Mr. Kinsman. I am Sheriff Torgeson."

Uncle Harry leaned across his desk. "How do you do, Sir. I am likewise pleased to meet you."

The two shook hands warmly and turned to me. Before Uncle Harry could comment, TJ came to me.

"Ah! Casey Jones," he beamed. "I am delighted to see you again." He shook my hand for several seconds. "Truly a fine piece of work you did down in Oregon!"

"Thank you Sir."

He turned back to Uncle Harry. "This amazing young man has guts, suh. Picked up on the trail of a wanted criminal where I left off, got some help, and captured him, no less. A true credit to your family, suh. Yes, indeed, Jones here is a nephew to be proud of!"

Just minutes after Uncle Harry had scolded me, we now heard the deputy sheriff giving me accolades of high praise.

"Ah hum," Uncle Harry sputtered. "Well, I hear the Troaz episode ended well."

"Indeed it did! My yes! It ended with that fierce outlaw in custody. Entirely because Jones here, like a professional lawman, continued on up to the bushwhacker's hideout, found his hidden loot and promptly turned it all in to the proper authorities."

Now, waving TJ to a chair, Uncle Harry offered him a cigar and, after both men had lighted them, the conversation continued.

Uncle Harry raised his eyebrows. "You mentioned stolen property."

"Yes. It consisted of three packets. Two remain with the Umatilla County Sheriff in Oregon while Troaz awaits trial. But Jones, here, was authorized to transport the third packet, one containing coins, to me for immediate restitution."

"Restitution?"

"Yes Sir." Deputy Torgeson leaned back and waved his cigar. "Ya see, jus' a couple a weeks ago, Troaz on his way through these parts, havin' crossed over the mountains from Tacoma, stopped at the Jesse Crisp place some five miles west of here. Mr. Crisp agreed to let Troaz spend the night in the barn . . . even invited him to dinner."

"Like the Connors did for us in Oregon," I added.

"Exactly. However, offering hospitality to Virgil Troaz turned out to be the first mistake for the Crisps," said the deputy, while puffing his cigar.

"While chattin' over the meal, Mrs. Crisp committed the biggest blunder. She mentioned that they'd jus' come up from Oregon to retire on their little cattle ranch there after sellin' their salmon business down on the Columbia."

TJ obviously enjoying the telling of it, continued the story.

"You might guess what happened next. When Troaz heard that the Crisps had jus' sold their business, he rightly figured there'd be some cash around the place. He jumped up from the table whipped out his huntin' knife and threatened to cut Mrs. Crisp's throat if they didn't produce their stash."

Uncle Harry leaned forward as I asked the obvious question. "How did the Crisps live through that?"

TJ knocked ash from his cigar. "Well, just after Mr. Crisp handed over the pouch o' gold coins, Troaz couldn't resist takin' a peek at the contents and loosened his grip on The Missus. At that, Jesse saw his chance to make his move.

"Still tough as whalebone, the older man jumped Troaz, knocking him to the floor. But the outlaw, quick as a cat, rolled over, and with pouch in hand, escaped by diving through an open window. Mrs. Crisp fetched their shotgun, but Virgil Troaz got clean away."

Uncle Harry, obviously impressed by the story, remarked, "Quite extraordinary!"

Then, with a steely stare, Uncle Harry came down to business. "I have not had the opportunity to examine the contents of the pouch that Casey entrusted to my safekeeping. Tell me, Torgeson, exactly what is the value of the coins in question?"

T.J. Torgeson sat straight as a ramrod. "The Umatilla County Sheriff has verified Jesse Crisp's contention that the pouch contains coins worth exactly thirty seven hundred dollars."

Uncle Harry sat forward, slapping his desk with both hands.

"Thirty seven hundred dollars! Good Lord man! That's a small fortune! Far too much for one young man to carry on the trail."

Then, looking sternly at me, "Casey, were you aware of the huge sum of money entrusted to you?"

"Yes sir, I signed for it in front of the sheriff."

Rising to his feet, Uncle Harry forcefully ground out his cigar.

"Sheriff Torgeson, am I to understand that it was by your order that this was done?"

"Yes suh, it was."

"How can you possibly justify such an action which, rightly considered, put the coins at risk of being stolen on the way, thereby placing my nephew in serious jeopardy."

T.J. Torgeson seemed unperturbed at the verbal challenge. Carefully placing his cigar in the tray, he calmly met Uncle Harry's glare.

"I stand by my decision . . . and ask you suh to see the logic of acting quickly, before Troaz, who was in jail, could arrange an attack by someone on the outside. Then too, a young man riding alone would be least suspected of carrying a huge sum of money."

Uncle Harry sat back, removed his glasses, and stared out the window.

"Very well, I do see your reasoning; however, I feel you took advantage of my nephew."

"Possibly I did. But Jones, here, proved himself many times over to be a young man of rare honesty and courage . . . one eager to see justice done."

Uncle Harry sighed and put his glasses back on. "How do you plan to return the coins to Mr. and Mrs. Crisp?"

"It is my intention to ride out and return the coin pouch to them before noon tomorrow."

Uncle Harry rose to his feet. "Since Casey has signed for the coins, legally he is still responsible for them. I suggest a different plan. He and I will leave with you immediately. We'll take you and the coins to the home of a friend of mine who is president of the Arborville Bank."

"Well, Mr. Kinsman, I acted quickly to get the coin pouch here, and now I'm obliged to respect your plan to safeguard it. But first we must verify the amount in the pouch."

"Yes indeed, we must verify the exact amount for all concerned. And who better to officially witness the counting of the coins, besides yourself, than a bank official?"

Torgeson looked dubious. "There is one drawback to your plan, Mr. Kinsman."

"What might that be?"

"Jesse Crisp doesn't deal with banks or bankers. He doesn't trust them."

At that Uncle Harry exploded. "Fire and brimstone! It's true that banks haven't a one hundred percent record of safeguarding funds entrusted to them, but our local bank is as safe as they come. One would think that having been robbed of their fortune in a life threatening manner, the Crisps would see the light."

Now Torgeson's smile matched the perpetual upturn of his mustache.

"True, quite true." The deputy jumped to his feet. "My automobile awaits in your driveway. Lead the way, Suh."

Having retrieved the Crisp's coin pouch on the way to the sheriff's car, Uncle Harry also picked up a small shotgun for our safety. When we reached the Model T Ford, I wasn't surprised to see TJ strap on a Colt 45 pistol. Despite the talk of robbery, I felt quite safe as we drove the six blocks to the banker's house.

Uncle Harry jumped out and in a few seconds we were welcomed and invited inside by tall, gray-haired Mr. Knox, at whose dining room table the coins were counted and the full amount verified. Inwardly I gave a sigh of relief as we all signed a legal paper to that effect.

My uncle thanked banker Knox and made a further request. "Now I must ask another favor. With the permission of the Sheriff, would you please unlock the bank and allow us to place this pouch in a safety deposit box?"

Mr. Knox agreed, as did T.J. Torgeson who, as we parted company, commented, "I'll ride out tomorrow and tell Jesse Crisp and his Missus, they'll jus' have to come in to the bank if they want to take their money home."

nineteen

THE SALMON MAN'S SURPRISE

The next day, a Monday, I put off a return to school one more day. By afternoon, I'd caught up on my rest.

I found a book on the Oregon Trail in the Overton Manor library and took a comfortable chair by the window. Fresh from my outdoor adventures on Oregon trails, I was totally immersed in the travails of pioneers, when a buggy drawn by two beautiful black horses glided up the driveway and stopped at the walkway beyond the front door.

Seconds later a middle-aged man and woman dressed in their Sunday clothes rang the doorbell.

Sally the maid came to me.

"Casey, there's a couple here to see you."

"Please show them in."

Minutes later, Mr. and Mrs. Crisp had introduced themselves, refused the offer of coffee, and sat down opposite me in comfortable chairs. The couple looked me over and Mr. Crisp quickly began.

"First off, the sheriff's deputy told us that we have you to thank for the safe return of our coins. Quite remarkable what you did. And now that we've met you, it's hard to believe that a boy still in school could have brought Virgil Troaz in."

"It is! It's just hard to believe!" said Mrs. Crisp, the tassels on her lavender hat shaking in agreement. "We had given up on ever getting a penny of our money back from that dangerous man."

"Without the help of several others I would have failed."

Mr. Crisp nodded. "Yes, but from what we've heard from T.J. Torgeson who'd given up the chase, without your stubborn decision not to give up, there'd a been no happy ending for us. "

"Thanks for your kind words." I said, feeling uncomfortable.

"But we're not here with just words." Mrs. Crisp stated with arched eyebrows.

"That's right." Mr. Crisp handed me a small leather bag. "We want you to have this . . . by way of underscoring our gratitude."

I took the bag and emptied five shiny twenty-dollar gold pieces into my hand.

"Skidoo! Thank you very much, but I don't feel right about taking this from you. You must know that the main reason I continued after Virgil Troaz was because he'd stolen my horse."

Mr. Crisp shook his finger at me. "Now, young man, we insist you take this small part of what was returned to us. You have your whole life ahead of you. It's time you built your future. Take my advice. Invest this little windfall. Used in the right way, it could make a nice difference some day."

What a surprise! I accepted the coins with thanks.

Before the Crisps left, they told a fascinating true story of how forty-two years earlier, they'd traveled west on the Oregon Trail from Council Bluffs Iowa. After three months of walking by their wagon they'd arrived at the Columbia River.

So impressed were they by the Native Americans fishing at Celilo Falls, they'd set up camp nearby with a wagon load of canned goods and trading items they'd brought with them.

They did well from the beginning. The natives wanted to buy their goods and paid for them in salmon that had been cured in a process of cleaning, drying and smoking with a touch of salt. The Crisps called this delicious product, Kippered Salmon.

The Crisps were barely twenty years old when they began. The business grew through the years as they sold salmon in the stores of Portland and bought more goods to replenish their little trading post.

As Mrs. Crisp concluded her story, she smiled. "Yes, Kippered Salmon kept and shipped well. When the railroad came through, we developed customers all over the northwest and as far east as Chicago."

Mr. Crisp with a satisfied smile looked kindly at me. "We've learned a lesson the hard way. We will leave our money in the bank. We'll even let Mr. Knox invest it so folks can borrow money to start their own business as we did. That way we'll get a bit of interest on our savings."

Just before they rode away, the Crisps insisted that I pay them a visit.

"Casey, we like you. Our little ranch is on the way to the main trail south. If you're down our way, stop in for a meal and a chat. We have a spare bedroom too, should you want to stay over."

When Uncle Harry arrived home from The Northern Pacific depot, I told him of the Crisps visit and their gift of coins to me.

"Well, congratulations Casey. What are your plans for the hundred dollars?"

"Do you have any investment suggestions."

"I do," he replied. "You encouraged our relatives in Seattle to find a way to sell the waste from their canning operation.

"In the very way you suggested, and with my financial help, they are drying and packaging salmon waste as high quality fertilizer. At the moment, we need to advertise and expand the sale of this product. I recommend that you use your coins as collateral at the bank in order to help us promote our product."

"Skiddoo! That's a great idea!" I said as I handed over the bag of coins.

"Consider it done!" said Uncle Harry with one of his broadest smiles.

twenty

MEETING DANGER HEAD-ON

I welcomed settling into classes and the routine of school again. What had begun as an overnight jaunt on Jasper to the Columbia Gorge and back had turned out to be an experience way beyond what I could have imagined. For several days the whirl of catching up on what I'd missed at school pushed everything else out of my mind.

I'd gone to a basketball game with Neva and had felt self-conscious about having a cast on my arm. On the way out of the gym, it got worse. A classmate, Jerry Conance came up and greeted us. He flashed a handsome smile at Neva and turned to me.

"Hey there, Casey, what's with the lame wing? Heard you fell off your horse. I guess New Yorkers just seem to have problems around horses."

I let the remark about being an easterner pass. Jerry had always been friendly, but now, seeing me with Neva, he seemed a bit jealous. Maybe the word had gotten around that the Kinsman girls weren't first cousins of mine.

"Hi Jerry, I replied." I didn't exactly fall off Jasper, but I don't pretend to be a rodeo star."

"Ha ha, well I guess not," he smirked. "Hey maybe Annie could give you some riding lessons."

"Well, she's a natural on a horse all right." This mild comment seemed to end the conversation and we left Jerry with a sour look on his face.

Following the unpleasantness with Jerry, except for school, I stayed at Overton Manor and dug into my homework. Lucky for me, even with my broken arm I could hold a pen, so did some of my own writing. Colette and Annie helped me with the rest.

I enjoyed being with the outgoing Kinsman girls who were so friendly with me. Even so, now and then my thoughts would return to the Connor family and especially to Louella. I missed her spirited ways, her rubbing liniment on my sore shoulder and her flashing eyes.

I yearned to get back to Oregon and wondered about April 10th, when we'd planned to travel up to the mysterious mountain man's home in the high valley.

What would Anton Hoffman have in store for us?

I longed to head back to the Connor's comfortable home, sit at their table sipping coffee, and go fishing again with Louella.

Before I knew it, we were into Christmas break, and I looked forward to getting my cast off.

This Christmas at Overton Manor the holiday was even more loving and joyful as the Kinsmans celebrated Our Savior's birth with presents under a beautifully decorated tree, wonderful food and the whole family singing carols every evening.

During Christmas break I caught up with all missed assignments. I was hesitant to participate in any of the usual after school activities because of my broken arm, so I threw myself into my studies and by the end of February, I'd worked ahead in all of my subjects.

Just before the end of the semester, the principal called me in. I was surprised to learn that due to the excellent New York school background, and the coursework from Daniel Webster High in Seattle, I had completed all of the graduation requirements early.

Since September I'd been spending my Saturdays at the depot, learning the basics of railroading and assisting the waybill clerk. But when Uncle Harry heard the news that my high school studies were complete, he suggested that I increase my learning schedule to six days a week.

I would rather have spent my spare time riding Jasper out in the cool breezes and visiting with Cal Paluskin up at his snowy Hideaway on the mountain. But now, winter snows had brought a mantle of white to the K2 high country.

Situated at the confluence of the Serpentine and the Columbia rivers, with direct rail connections to busy overseas ports of both Washington and Oregon, the Arborville rail yard had developed into a busy switching station.

Boxcars filled with timber, potatoes or sacks of grain were uncoupled one at a time from one train and switched over to another.

For several hours each day I busied myself with the paperwork that directed the amazingly smooth tracking of thousands of boxcars, gondola cars, cattle cars and flatcars filled with all kinds of wholesale goods being shipped to market.

I'd been helping the telegrapher and office manager during the day for five weeks when Uncle Harry switched me to the midnight to eight in the morning shift. This meant I would be helping with passenger trains.

At 1:30, the early morning passenger train going east stopped at Arborville. Then at 3:45, the westbound train pulled in.

Once as I watched the Seattle bound train come to a stop,

bell clanging, amidst a cloud of steam, I thought of that fateful afternoon when I'd arrived on this same platform. I'd been a scared kid of sixteen, and now I'd left childhood behind.

While passengers got off and on, I helped the telegrapher pull the wagons heaped high with baggage and U.S. Mail bags to the forward cars of these trains. It was heavy lifting, done under pressure of time.

By the time I'd arrived back at Overton Manor, I was exhausted from using my left arm for everything.

During my second week on night shift, while sitting at the clerk's desk, I fought to stay awake. I glanced up at the large pendulum clock. At ten minutes after four in the morning there were almost four dreary hours left of my shift.

I'd thought of learning to play checkers, the game that the night shift telegraphers, miles apart, played by wire during slack times. Complete with both red and black checkers, numbered boards would be set up in train stations along the way.

When a pair of telegraphers agreed to play each other, two numbers would be telegraphed for each move. The first number identified the checker's spot before the move, and the second number told where to move it.

Harv Tiller the young telegrapher on night shift was a good checker player. During my mid-shift break, I would chat with Harv and it was fun for me to watch him play by telegraph. He'd make his move, telegraph it, and wait for the man down the line to send his move back.

One night the telegraph in the next office began its string of clicks, but it wasn't some other telegrapher wanting to play checkers. It was the train dispatcher about to send orders for the next freight train. Harv would decode it, and minutes later, would hand up the written order to the train crew as the freight passed by non-stop.

With one main set of tracks, those orders from the dispatcher prevented trains running in opposite directions from colliding head-on with each other. One train would wait on a siding while another would pass by on the main line. These orders also insured a clear main track through the two mile yard limits through town. The local switch engine crews who were busy routing and spotting cars for pick up, had to stay on the sidings when trains came through.

I'd become accustomed to the clicking sound of the telegraph. In fact, on this night, it's clicking was about to lull me to sleep when I heard Harv's terrifying shout.

"My God!" he yelled. "The freight's ahead of schedule, it's just a mile up the track, and the switch engine pulling a line of cars hasn't cleared the main line yet!"

In a flash I visualized a massive train wreck as the oncoming freight train's huge steam locomotive crashed into the freight cars of the local train that hadn't yet fully pulled onto the siding. It would be a re-play of the famous crash of twenty years back.

On that occasion, my namesake, Illinois Central engineer Casey Jones, had realized too late that the local train ahead needed a few more minutes to clear the track.

Casey Jones had prided himself in making such fast time, that he'd named his locomotive "The Cannonball." On this occasion, when the engineer had seen boxcars on the tracks ahead, he was unable to stop his train in time. Casey Jones died in that train wreck.

Maybe Harv had similar thoughts as he ran to the emergency equipment shelf calling out, "Torpedoes! Torpedoes!" Wild-eyed with fear, he threw three torpedoes, mounds covered with red paper and filled with gunpowder, on the table. Each measured two inches across and included a piece of flat wire at the base.

As he ran to the door, he shouted, "Quick, fasten those to

the rail. I'll run up the track to flag the freight down!"

With that, he bolted out the door with a red lantern in his hand.

I'd read in the Railroad Book of Rules what to do in such an emergency. Besides swinging a red lantern, a train could be signaled to stop by attaching three torpedoes to the rail spaced fifty feet apart. As the engine ran over them, each in turn would explode with a loud report. The engineer would hear the three torpedoes sounding off, and would set the brakes and stop as soon as possible.

Never had I missed the use of my right arm so much as now! I slipped two of the torpedoes into my coat pocket and frantically grasped the third in my left hand heading for the main line that lay forty feet from the depot door.

As I fell to my knees, I heard the freight train's engine whistle screaming it's routine warning for the crossing just east of town. The thought seared my mind. "It's only a mile away and going about a mile a minute!"

I placed the first torpedo on the rail. Hampered by my own shadow from the station lights, I tried to see the flat wire attached underneath the torpedo.

"Ah!" I thought as I got one side bent down. But then, the torpedo fell off between the rails.

In a frenzy now, my trembling fingers found the torpedo, and again fitted it on the track. Then, with my forehead holding the powder-filled object down on the rail, I secured the wires.

"There's one!" I shouted. As I scrambled on up the track trying to judge fifty feet for the placement of the second one, I heard the engine whistle at the crossing and I prayed that Harv was there waving his red lantern.

More quickly this time, I attached the second torpedo and, as I ran to the third position, I could hear the thunderous roar of the locomotive charging up to me. Had the engineer seen Harv's lantern?

Once again, I had to attach a torpedo holding it to the rail with my head, which could be squashed like a pumpkin by the on-rushing juggernaut. The platform quaked as I struggled with the wires.

Was the freight slowing? If not, at sixty miles an hour, the train would be steaming along at EIGHTY EIGHT FEET A SECOND. By the time I would hear the first torpedo explode, just a mere hundred feet up the track, it would be too late to pull back! The locomotive would be upon me!

I finished attaching the last device and fell back just a few seconds before the BANG! BANG! BANG! of exploding torpedoes.

A deafening screech of brakes filled the air and I continued to scramble back amid a shower of sparks from the wheels.

I'd done it. I sat panting, heart pounding . . . praying that the train would stop in time . . . and in less than a minute it did.

I heard no crash of rending metal, no grinding sound of the engine plowing into freight cars.

With a sigh of relief, I ran up the tracks for half a mile until I came to the head end of the train. It had stopped mere feet short of contact with the boxcars that were still slowly moving onto the siding.

As they cleared the tracks of the main line, the brakeman rushed over and thew the switch, clearing the way on the main line for the train that had screeched to an emergency stop.

Harv came running. On the way back he'd stopped long enough to grab the orders at his desk and ran to the head of the train and handed them up to the wide-eyed engineer.

"Move on out! Stay on schedule!" he shouted breathlessly. And the train began to move forward again.

As we trotted back to the station, the telegrapher handed up a copy of the orders to the conductor as the caboose went by. Then Harv turned and shook his head in disbelief.

"Casey, train wrecks don't come any closer than that!"

An hour later, after a flurry of messages with the dispatcher, things settled down in the depot.

Harv and I sat looking at each other. Still tensed up from the close call, Harv remarked. "We made history here tonight . . . but this time Casey Jones saved the day."

I was speechless, unable to respond.

Never had I felt so close to my namesake, the valiant engineer who'd tried to avoid a train wreck. In death he'd become a folk hero. A popular song had been written in his honor.

No one would write a song about what happened here in Arborville tonight, but I knew that for years to come I'd feel good inside. Harvey Tiller and I had stopped mighty forces from violently smashing together.

twenty- one

THE VIEW AHEAD

y part in avoiding a train wreck caused a stir in Arboville, but a little less than I expected. The local Arborville Grapevine newspaper ran a low-key article on page five.

It simply read:

Collision Avoided - Coincidence Noted

At 4:23 this morning, a collision between a west bound freight train and boxcars pulled by the local switch engine was averted by the fast work of Casey Jones, a night clerk at the Arborville Northern Pacific depot. Jones set warning torpedoes on the track that signaled the engineer of the oncoming freight to stop just in time. Some twenty years ago, another Casey Jones, an engineer for the Illinois Central, unlike our railroader, was unable to avoid a train wreck under similar conditions and died in that crash.

Uncle Harry was beside himself with glee, bursting with pride as he spoke to others about my fast work.

At nine the next morning I was asleep when he came into my bedroom. He woke me up by announcing in a loud voice,

"Casey, I just came from my office. The place is abuzz with praise for you. I just can't believe you acted so quickly to set those torpedoes . . . and you did it with one arm! Amazing! Astonishing! You have my heartiest congratulations."

"Thanks, Uncle Harry," I replied, rubbing sleep from my eyes. "But it was Harv Tiller who got the torpedoes out . . . his idea to set them."

"It's good of you to share the credit, but he should have set them on the track himself and let you take the red lantern forward."

Then, still beaming, Uncle Harry continued. "But that's hindsight. No one blames Harv. He did a lot of things right. It turns out the engineer did see his red lantern. Also Harv quickly got the train going again and, in doing so, probably saved a snarl in the flow of trains. You and Harv Tiller will both receive official commendations from our head office."

That evening, at the Kinsman dinner table, I enjoyed the conversation much as usual. After Uncle Harry led us in giving thanks, Colette was first with her usual quick comment.

"Casey, the kids at school didn't talk about anything else today. Good golly! Stopping a train! We just can't believe how cool headed you were!"

"Well, I just followed the night man's orders."

"Ha! Your face is getting red, Casey," said Neva with one of her sideways looks.

Annie piped up. "Casey, we're so proud of you! I can't imagine what it would be like to run out in the dark and put those explosive things on the track with a train rushing at you."

Uncle Harry gave me a warm look. "You should all know just how heroic a thing it was. Casey risked his life out there."

"Well, thanks Uncle Harry, but there's one thing about last night that makes me smile. Just a minute before all the excitement, I was dozing at my desk, bored with my railroad job and longing for a little action."

That brought laughter from all and Aunt Louise commented, "That's proof that one should be a bit cautious about what you wish for."

"That's certainly true, my dear," said Uncle Harry. "But Casey, you have been wanting to get the cast off your arm and tomorrow's the day."

At that, I pumped my left arm and cheered, "Skidoo! Yea! At last!"

I'd been given time off from my railroad training, so I had a good night's sleep before going to the doctor and watching him remove the cast. I had expected my arm to be discolored, but it looked surprisingly normal, and it felt fairly strong too.

At last, I had two good arms!

twenty-two

THE HIGH COUNTRY

The next day I was back riding Jasper, taking in the wonder of the early spring sounds that floated across the fields. The call of the hawk mingled with the braying of cattle.

I loved the cool, pine-scented air that drifted down from the woods. Once again I was deeply charged with an electric sense of wellbeing, a sensation I'd never known before coming west to live.

Cal Paluskin waited up on the hill. We planned to trail though the woods looking for elk that would be heading for the high country. Beautiful animals, I'd never spotted one before. Except . . . on that almost unreal experience when I'd found the mountain man, Anton Hoffman, pinned under his wagon on the whitewater trail. A short horned elk had been harnessed to that wagon. The recollection now seemed more like a dream than reality.

The thought of seeing elk out here gave me an emotional rush. With Cal as my guide we would observe them in their habitat, then we'd ride back to the Hideaway for one of Cal's meals cooked over the open fire. This evening we'd plan a trip together.

I'd heard of the area to the northwest, the North Cascades . . . beautiful and wild, with a chain of lakes fed by melting snow.

Another possible late-spring trip, the wild Klickitat area lay just overland to the west. Cal described its river, teeming with trout. It descended rapidly through pristine woodlands to join the Columbia near Celilo Falls.

I was attracted to the Klickitat River, and its excellent fishing. Cal opted for the northern territory with the opportunity for canoeing. How to decide? This evening, over coffee, we'd watch the campfire cast its dancing shadows and discuss the possibilities. I looked forward to the friendly discussion.

We had time to decide. The ideal time for the woodsy trek would be late spring. But I sensed Cal wanted a decision.

Now, in early afternoon, I leaned back in the saddle and announced our arrival with the usual birdcall. When it was quickly returned I knew Cal awaited us at the Hideaway.

Cal had coffee ready as I rode in. He'd patted Jasper's flank and greeted me with, "Good to see you, and Jasper too." But as we sat by the fire, he seemed eager to get on the trail of the elk.

"I heard them this morning. Each big male stakes out a part of the woods."

As we chewed a snack of venison jerky I felt the excitement of catching sight of the Northwest's largest animal, second in size only to the moose found further north.

"So the male picks a territory and hopes the females will join him?" I asked.

"Yes. The male makes a sound hunters call bugling . . . very loud. It is a warning to other males in the area to stay away. We will hear it today."

Soon we were guiding our horses slowly along a side hill

trail, heading for the upper range of forest. Within minutes we noted elk droppings and Cal pointed to areas of greenery that contained bare stems. Cal pointed out these signs of feeding and also where hooves had scratched lichen from fallen trees.

"Will the elk run if they see us?" I asked.

"Yes, but if we're careful that won't happen. We have a favorable breeze; the elk are upwind from us. Our scent could stir up the male elk. This time of year one might even charge us."

Then suddenly I heard a male bugling and a thrill charged through me. The strange sound began with a low moan and rose to a very loud series of clear, rapidly alternating high notes before dropping down again . . . ending with last-breath grunts.

Cal smiled. "That one is near. He sounds big . . . maybe a thousand pounds. He could be ten feet with antler."

Skidoo! Ten feet tall! I silently prayed that no elk with huge antlers would challenge us.

We stopped in a small clearing and Cal pointed to a grassy knoll up ahead. There, in a circle of light, stood the huge animal. And once again he bellowed out his clarion call of the wilderness . . . its spine-tingling sound rolled through the forest.

"Skidoo," I thought, as I caught my breath. "That mighty sound should ward off other males and attract female elk as well."

Yes, this stately animal, with his rack of antlers, was the most impressive thing I'd seen in the woods.

To avoid disturbing the elk, we withdrew and circled up and around for half a mile. Then we dismounted and gazed down on nine elk as they grazed in a little high country meadow. Just above on a rock ledge stood the huge male.

As shadows lengthened, Cal and I rode back to the Hideaway.

"I didn't expect the elk to be so big, especially the male."

"Uhunh. For one so large, brother elk runs swiftly . . . moving through the trees like the wind. Guided by his mighty spirit, his antlers touch nothing."

Warmed by a blazing campfire, we finished our meal of roast rabbit and sipped wild mint tea. Cal mentioned a few details of the elk's migration to the high country then began to speak of our spring hike.

"In late spring when we finish branding the young stock, Bernie will give me some time off. You and I can ride to some-place where we can fish, and maybe paddle a canoe."

"I've never traveled by canoe, but I think I'd like it."

"Uhuuh, in the lakes of the north Cascades, you would like it."

I slowly sipped my tea, and luxuriously stretched out on a bearskin, leaning on the log behind me.

"The farm in Oregon where I stayed had a trout stream nearby."

"Did you get to it?"

"Yes, but I only caught one."

At this, I detected a flicker of a smile. "Uhunh, sometimes it's like that . . . fish not want to take bait."

"That was it. The girl who lived there began to catch one right after another with waterbug bait. I switched over to it and caught a big one."

"Uhunh, if we go up north, we will catch plenty fish . . . plenty every day."

Once again I just lolled back, gave a sigh and said, "But I hear the Klickitat River is full of trout."

"That is true, plenty fish there too, but no canoeing . . . too much whitewater along it."

"For our spring trek, you favor heading north, then?"

"I do."

"When I was on the Columbia, I saw where the Klickitat

flows in. I would like to see it farther up, where it rises in timber. I favor heading west to fish its upper waters."

"Uhunh, how do you want to decide it?"

I paused for another sip from my tin cup. "An easy way would be to flip a coin, but I don't happen to have one with me."

"How then?"

"Well," I drawled. "We could rassle. The winner gets to decide."

"Uhunh." Cal leaned forward and looked intently. "Your arm . . . it is all right?"

"Good as new."

"Umm. I only know the way . . . as my native brothers wrestle."

"How's that?"

Cal's dark eyes shone in the firelight. "Anything goes."

Thinking back to my wrestling in New York, I raised an eyebrow. "Anything? Gouging and kneeing too?"

"No! Not that."

"How do you know who wins . . . when a match is over?"

"That is the same all over, I think . . . shoulders pinned to ground. Match over then, unless we say two out of three falls."

"O.K. Are you ready now?"

"We will wait until sunup tomorrow to wrestle."

"Good idea, I'm too full of food right now."

"Uhunh. Just before we make morning fire we will hear this . . . Whoo whoo whooo . . . the last cry of the night owl. And then we will hear the early call of the red-winged blackbird and know it is time to begin our contest."

We rolled into our blankets, but before the fire died down, Cal returned to it, kneeling on a bearskin before the flickering embers.

Then I heard the low moan of an eerie chant. In the dim light I felt intimidated. With his face contorted into a fierce expression, Cal was mentally preparing himself for the wrestling match with me.

This went on for a few more minutes. Then he sliced a bit of fur from the bearskin, sprinkling the hair from it into the fire. With head back, he lifted his arms to the rising smoke before returning to his blanket.

The next morning the sun cast a pale glow as I trotted down to wash in the spring-fed stream. Cal was up, his bare chest glistening in the sun's early rays. He'd been toning his muscles by lifting a chunk of cedar that we sometimes used as a footstool.

He tossed it aside and I thought of the bible quotation, "and I shall make him your footstool." The fierce expression on Cal's face made me feel that I was about to get the footstool treatment from him.

I wiped my face and arms with my shirt and cast it aside. Cal in buckskin pants planted his bare feet in the earth and crouched before me. I removed my moccasins and wiped my hands on my denim pants.

Just as I stood before him in a similar crouch, I barely had time to tense up before the sweet song of the red-winged blackbird began our match of strength and skill.

What had begun as a suggestion for a friendly way to settle a difference between us, now had become a fierce test of will; I felt a flame of fear rise up. I might be humbled more than I would want. With Cal, I would lose some of his respect if I made a miserable showing. I wouldn't want to fall in his regard for me.

But I'd met challenges before . . . such as when, some six months ago, I'd been thrust into a stoker's job on a fishing boat. My muscles were still well developed from shoveling coal back then. And I'd been able to hold off Virgil Troaz.

I respected Cal's serious mental preparation, and I prayed to be a worthy match for him!

We began to circle each other. With quick footwork, we stepped forward and back, sparring for a handhold. Then suddenly, Cal charged, head down. I'd anticipated this. I grasped his shoulders and fell back, knees up, flipping him over me as I landed on my back.

We both sprang to our feet, but went down together as Cal took me off my feet with a second charge. I twisted as we fell, landing on top.

Though Cal was five years older, I was a few pounds heavier. His skill and strength forced me to roll, and then, as I regained the upper hand, we rolled again so that neither of us could pin the others shoulders to the ground.

This continued for several seconds. Then Cal twisted a leg around one of mine using his foot as a lever to turn me over. He worked his arms around my waist in a fierce bear-hug that pinned my left arm.

Short of breath, I felt my strength ebbing away, my shoulders began to turn. I gave one last effort to get free, but Cal pinned me to the ground and I managed to say "give".

Later, after a simple breakfast, I commented, "Cal, you're stronger than I thought. Back east, I wrestled some older and bigger guys. I had more than my share of wins, especially with boys my size. I can't remember being beaten by someone even slightly smaller, until today."

"Uhunh, you fought well, like the fierce badger, but I had strength from the mighty brown bear."

twenty-three

UNEXPECTED ADVENTURE

*U*ncle Harry arranged for me to join four other K2 ranch hands as we drove a herd of a hundred and fifty cattle, twenty miles to the rail yard.

It was a dusty job, but I got deep satisfaction from it . . . sleeping under the stars and eating meals from the chuck wagon prepared by one of our drovers, Sut Fritipan, who doubled as cook. I was sorry it only lasted one night and a couple of days.

Sut, the oldest cowboy among us, told true stories of other cattle drives. As we sat around the campfire, he painted mental pictures of the southwest, on the Skimerhorn Trail and down along the Cimarron.

In earlier times, driving large herds of Longhorn cattle might involve weeks of overland travel, with the cowboys constantly contending with challenges, some ending in catastrophe.

They found some river crossings so swift, the whitewater would carry off a steer, while other rivers posed no problem. "The Pecos," Sut claimed, "ran an inch deep and a mile wide."

With all eyes on him, Sut tossed another chunk of wood on

the fire, causing an explosion of sparks that rose in the black night like a huge swarm of fireflies.

Our trail boss, Bernie Wellman, asked, "Sut, what was the worst thing that ever happened to you on a drive?"

"Well, once down Texas way, we had more'n our share of things go wrong. One time 'bout three days south of the Panhandle, after a day with sun so hot it'd like to fry a sidewinder, we noticed a heavy feelin' in the air. We saw a black cloud aformin' in the west and figger'd we were in for it.

"Cattle get jumpy when the 'lectricity builds . . . it puts a charge on things, and yer hair stands up. Ya can tell somethin's 'bout to happen, 'cause everything gets real quiet . . . not even a nicker from the hosses."

Without thinking, as Sut paused, we all leaned forward.

"Trail boss, he didn't need to say nothin' to us. We knew to spread out on the flanks of the herd . . . soft talkin' 'em. My trail buddy, Billy, and I we went farther out, so's we had drovers all around the herd, in case of trouble."

As Sut described the approaching storm we imagined a prairie tragedy in the making.

"Thing of it was, we didn't hear much thunder until the clouds were almost overhead. Then, CRACK, the flash and the thunder came at the same time."

Sut looked down and shook is head, remembering.

"Them steers like ta jumped straight up offun the ground, then cut loose in all directions. There was no headin' off a stampede as they scattered.

"We were between a rock and a hard place all right. Steada trying to head 'em off, we wound up ridin' to save our skins."

There was too long a pause, and I asked, "And did you? Did you all get out of it alive?"

Sut shook his head. "The next day we rounded up most of

the herd . . . all but 'bout twenty head that we never did see agin' . . . they may be runnin' yet fer all I know.

"But the worst of it was that Billy and his hoss got caught . . . trampled into the dust along with ten head that fell over 'em and went down too.

"We did bury Billy out there . . . under his ripped up saddle.

"There's a cowboy song that kinda sings for Billy."

Sut looked at me, and after a few minutes of somber reflection on the life of the cowboy, I tuned up my guitar and began to softly play.

"O bury meee,

On the lone prairieee,

Where the coyotes howl,

And the wind blows freee."

I followed with,

"As I walked out on the streets of Loredo,

On the streets of Loredo, I walked out one day."

This picked up the mood and I followed in with, Tumbling Tumbleweed and The Big Rock Candy Mountain, but Sut's tale of Bill being trampled to death on the trail lingered on, as those of us not keeping watch slowly moved to curl up in our bedrolls.

Snug in my blankets, I gazed up at the bright stars and pondered anew the legend of the cowboy. While Sut had told his tale of hazards on the trail, I'd been drawn into the folklore of the West. Now thoughts of gunfights, rustlers and stampeding cattle swirled in my head.

On this drive I'd become a part of the drover's dusty and dangerous way of life. With peace and contentment I drifted off to sleep amid the lowing of cattle and the odor of sagebrush.

On the last day, time lagged as Jasper and I traveled at the plodding speed of the cattle. We couldn't hurry them and I had time to think ahead.

In just three days Jasper and I would travel back to the Connor farm. I'd arrive a couple of days early for a nice visit, like Louella suggested.

I wondered what interesting adventure awaited us on April 10th when we'd ride to the mountain man's mysterious place that lay somewhere across the whitewater crossing.

Anton Hoffman had promised to return Dublin to me. But what else did the man of mystery have in store for us? I could hardly wait to find out!

By mid-afternoon, all hundred and fifty head of cattle had been run into the stockyard at the railhead and Bernie had received the first payment and a signed receipt for them.

Returning to Jasper, I heard Bernie call out, "Listen up boys, there'll be no chuck wagon meal for us jus' now."

Startled by this, I stammered, "Well, how come?"

"Because Mr. Kinsman has allowed us a bonus. He's springing for a full meal. Dinner'll be at the Ranchers and Rustlers Restaurant across the way there."

What a pleasant surprise! As the boys strode down the street, they yelled: "Whoooeee! and "Ki yi yippee-yippee-yay!"

The boys and I didn't hold back. We ordered thick steaks, big baked potatoes and fresh cut asparagus along with endless pots of coffee. Driving cattle had whetted my appetite. What a delicious meal!

I joined in the trail talk and laughter, but as we were finishing the last of the apple pie dessert, I noticed a copy of the Arborville Grapevine on a nearby table and my eye caught the title of an article on the front page.

DESPARADO ESCAPES
Convict in Daring Jailbreak!
I read the details, and almost got sick to my stomach.

Virgil Troaz had overpowered a guard and had ridden off on a stolen horse.

I quickly tossed the newspaper on a chair and forced a smile. I didn't mention the serious news to the fellas. Why take away their happy mood. Instead, I stood up to leave.

"I guess you all will be bedding down in camp, but if I leave now, I'll be back at Overton Manor before dark."

"O.K., Casey," Sut drawled with a wink at the others. "We know how it is with city slickers. After one night on the trail, they hanker fer a soft bed."

As I left, Bernie caught up to me. "Casey, the boys'll be moseying over to the saloon to wash some the dust out of their throats, but I'm headin' to our camp. I got a down payment of a seventy five dollars for the cattle. Would you take it to yer Uncle Harry tonight?"

I replied, "Sure I'll get it to him."

I put the cash in the pouch I carried around my neck. I already had twenty-five to take along for the ride to the Connors coming up. I thought, "That makes an even hundred."

I felt uneasy traveling with so much cash. But after all, I'd be back safe at Overton Manor before dark.

As the sun dipped low, Jasper and I headed out of town on the dirt road to Arborville. We'd loped along for perhaps ten miles when a rock bounced down from up above. It was so similar to the happening down on the Columbia River that it was just plain eerie. Had Troaz once again rolled the rock from up above?

I pulled Jasper around and headed back to the Serpentine. It would take an extra hour, but Jasper and I could circle back, cross at the wood bridge and still get home tonight.

Had Virgil Troaz actually rolled that rock onto the trail? I didn't really know, but I rode hard. I figured thirty miles to go now, and I was scared.

I glanced at the setting sun. Riding in the dark with the possibility of a desperate outlaw on my trail sent a shiver of fear up my spine.

As we topped a rise, I glanced back, and to my horror, spotted a rider in a long black cape riding swiftly behind us.

I spurred Jasper to full gallop, and now I had to fight down panic. Was it really Troaz, back there on my trail?

What would he do to me if he caught me out on this lonely stretch of road? I tried not to think about it.

Another few miles and I looked back again. Still dogging my tracks, the dark rider had actually gained on me, and I saw him whipping his horse to go faster.

Long shadows covered the road. With no moon to light the way, how would Jasper and I find our way to the Serpentine? We'd be forced to stop. I looked around for a farmhouse, but saw none.

I had no weapon except my knife. I recalled the warning in the article I'd read back at the restaurant . . . Caution! Armed and dangerous. Armed! Yes, he'd stolen a gun from his jailer!

I could barely see the road. After another half mile Jasper wandered off the roadway.

I dismounted and walked ahead, leading Jasper as we stumbled along in almost total darkness.

Then I blundered into a fence and fell, entangled in barbed wire. I got free but lost my direction. On hands and knees I felt for the edge of the road. Weeds and thistles stung my hands. I couldn't see or hear Jasper anywhere around.

I lay on my back, panting in frustration and fear. Just a few hours ago, back at the restaurant with a full stomach, I'd felt contented and satisfied on my first time out as a genuine cowpoke. I'd done the job, helped tend the herd and even lassoed a stray. I'd felt warm feelings from the K2 ranch hands.

Now, groveling in the weeds, fear seared my heart. How

could this disastrous turn of events have happened to me?

I calmed my breathing and, as part of a hazy plan, I reached back to the fence, brought out my knife and felt for a staple . . . one that fastened wire to the post. My fingers quickly guided the point of the knife as I pried loose the bent wire staple and slipped it in my shirt pocket.

I returned the knife to its sheath and heard sounds of a horse coming my way. I looked up and my brain froze . . . terrified as I made out a horse and rider dimly outlined against the night sky.

With no plan of escape, my breath came in sobs. I fought the urge to bolt . . . thrashing my way through the thistles.

Then I heard, "You sniveling brat. What did you do with my horse? Tell me quick or I'll beat it out of you."

It was Troaz!

I pulled my thoughts together. If I told the truth, that I'd left Dublin with the Mountain Man, I'd put kindly Anton Hoffman in danger. No! I had to string Troaz along in such a way that he would keep me alive.

So I said, "You're asking about your horse, the one I call Dublin. All right, I'll tell you. I sold him to the man who runs the ferry down on the Columbia."

"Sold my horse!"

"Yes, I got my horse back and the Umitilla sheriff gave Dublin to me. On the way back, the ferryman noticed I had an extra horse and offered me a hundred dollars for him and the saddle. I still have the money with me."

"You're nothing but a dang horse thief!"

"No! With you in jail, your horse was awarded to me for the trouble you caused."

At that, the outlaw jumped off and I scrambled to my feet.

"Trouble!" Troaz shouted as he grabbed my shirt. "You

haven't seen anything yet if we don't get me my horse back!"

In desperation I said, "Ride with me to the ferry!"

At that, Troaz produced a light rope and tied my hands behind my back. Surprised that he could see so well in the dark, I heard him bringing Jasper to me.

"Mount up. If you try anything, I'll shoot you dead."

Troaz led the way to the gorge. At the first rays of sunshine, we stopped and the outlaw untied me.

Black eyes flashing, the villain pulled out a pistol and aimed it at me.

"Now we have light enough to see. You'll either show me that hundred dollars cash you got for my horse or get a bullet between the eyes."

twenty-four

SHOWDOWN ON THE RIVER

Along with the drawstrings, a heavy rubber band secured the contents of my money pouch. Just before I handed the pouch to the outlaw, I pulled the band off and slipped it around my wrist.

Virgil Troaz holstered his gun and carefully counted the hundred dollars.

"Huh." He grunted. "Well, Jones, you're durn lucky. So far, your story checks out. You get to live a little longer."

Handing over the reins, he glared at me and brandished the pistol.

"You ride just ahead down to the ferry landing. Any sudden moves and I'll blast you with this .45."

I needed a plan of action.

The sun climbed higher as we followed the trail across grassy hills then down to the ferry landing.

I had a few minutes to decide how to make my move before Troaz challenged the unsuspecting ferryman.

In a daydream, I saw myself threatening Troaz with my knife and getting him to surrender. Hah! No chance of that.

But then I thought of a plan to take the desperado by

surprise.

Minutes later we watched as the tug and barge arrived in front of us.

I slipped the rubber band to my fingers to form a simple slingshot. Then I engaged the staple in the middle of the bands, ready to pull it back between the "V" of my fingers, waiting for just the right moment. The empty ferry docked and we rode on together.

How would Troaz's horse react when I let fly with a staple?

I aimed at an area of thick hide just forward of the horse's saddle, stretched the bands back several inches and let go.

Zap! The staple hit harmlessly, but to the horse it must have felt like a bee sting. He reared up, but Troaz held on.

This was my chance! I lunged for the outlaw, grabbing his cape as we both fell to the deck and landed with him facing away from me.

I got one arm under his shoulder and behind his head and, with the other, pinned his arm to his side. But Troaz was still able to pull his pistol and tried to shoot me in the leg.

As I grappled his legs with mine, he fired six shots and the last one did damage. I heard the ferryman yell and glanced up to see him grab his shoulder and fall on the deck.

Now Troaz pulled his gun arm free and began to pistol-whip me. I got a glancing blow to the head and ducked away to avoid another. I had my legs still locked around him so he whacked me with the gun barrel several times on my thigh in an effort to break my hold.

I noticed the ferryman sit up and I called to him, "Help! This man escaped from jail. Help me!"

And the ferryman did come to the rescue. Even with a wounded shoulder, he got up and kicked the pistol out of Troaz's hand. When I released and rolled away, the ferryman fell on the outlaw and knocked him out with one mighty swing of his fist.

I staggered back exhausted. My ears rang from being so close to the gun's loud reports and blood trickled down into my neck from the blow on my head.

Troaz's stolen horse had taken off back up the trail. Jasper had stayed on the barge and now stood snorting and stamping on the deck.

I sank down dazed and out of breath while the ferryman found a piece of rope and tied up the outlaw.

Then the wounded boatman glanced over his shoulder at two wagons waiting on the other side. Before I could stop him, he cast off and wildly swung the ferry out into the current.

Loss of blood from his shoulder wound must have affected his thinking. Heading back across was a foolish thing to do because, with one arm, the ferryman couldn't turn the wheel and called to me to help him.

I ran to the little wheelhouse as the current took the tugboat and barge. We began to swing around in large circles, whirling out of control.

The ferryman yelled, "Reverse the engine!" But I couldn't see how to do it. I became dizzy. He wildly tugged and turned the wheel, but for mile after mile we continued on.

In this nightmare come true, I could hear terrified Jasper neighing, calling to me to save us.

I yelled, "Celilo! How close are we to the falls?"

With terror in his eyes, the ferryman yelled, "We're comin' to it. Gotta get control or we'll wind up on the rocks below!"

"Where's the reverse lever?"

The ferryman with one arm dangling shouted and nodded, "Over there, black handle, pull it to the middle and then back."

Finally, I got the engine into reverse and with the tug's

steam engine huffing full astern, the whirling slowed. With a few turns of the wheel, we finally came around to an up-stream heading, but it was almost too late.

Crunch! The far end of the barge hit a submerged boulder near the head of the falls with a jarring lurch.

The ferryman yelled, "Full ahead now!"

I quickly responded and with the engine churning full ahead, we began to inch back upstream. We'd barely missed being swept over the falls. We'd avoided total disaster.

Heaving a sigh of relief, I looked around for Jasper.

But Jasper was gone! Probably knocked overboard when we'd hit the rock!

NO! NO! My tortured brain did not want to accept the terrible truth. I had lost my horse again!

I jumped up and ran to the rail, hoping not to see Jasper in the churning water below the falls.

But I did see him . . . floating in calmer water toward the Washington side.

"Put in to shore," I shouted. "My horse went over the falls."

The ferryman shook his head. "Can't! We'd hit more rocks."

"But he's probably injured! I've got to help him!"

The ferryman stared at the near shore. "I'll get us closer, but you'll have to swim for it."

And, as we drew nearer to shore, swim I did . . . with all my strength. Fortunately, the ferry had got us into an eddy, with a slower current near shore. Still, I feared being swept over the falls myself and put every ounce of strength into each stroke. I ignored my aching head and thigh and swam for my life.

Before jumping in, I'd taken off my boots, tied the laces together, and looped them around my neck. Still, I felt a drag from my clothes.

Several minutes later I felt the shore under my feet. Pulling myself onto the shore above the falls. I lay on my back, catching my breath for a few minutes before I found the strength to run down past the falls to the roiling waters below.

And there was poor Jasper, swimming weakly for shore, waters flowing about his large bulk.

I desperately ran down to riverbank, pushed a log from the shore into the current and held onto a projecting branch as I swam toward Jasper.

By paddling with one arm and with ferocious kicking I rode my makeshift riverboat, catching up to my valiant horse just as he came ashore and struggled to get up. After two tries, he'd managed to get only his front half out of the water and fell with his head on the shore. When I reached him, he lay snorting on a sandy spot of beach, his long tail floating in the water.

Horses sleep standing up, and I'd never seen Jasper lying down. Now I knelt beside him. When I heard him greet me with a little murmur, I burst into tears.

"Oh, Jasper," I sobbed in his ear. "Sorry I couldn't save you."

I rested my head on his neck and prayed, "Please don't let him die." But deep inside I knew that it would take a miracle to bring him back now.

I lost track of time. I raised my head and noticed a crimson trail in the water. I sensed that Jasper was bleeding to death. Twice he seemed to look at me. Then, just as the sun dipped behind a cloud, he closed his eyes for the last time. His big, powerful body stiffened in death. My heart broke as I held him tight.

The late afternoon sun had turned the sky to pale gold, reflecting in the calmer water downstream, but the natural beauty was wasted on me. A light breeze with its cool, fresh air filled my lungs, but didn't lift my spirits. Jasper lay dead in my arms.

In agony I sobbed, "Oh Jasper! How I will miss your flashing eyes, your nickering greeting for me . . . riding together swift as the wind."

twenty-five

SUNSET ON THE RIVER

*M*y fine neighbor in Brooklyn once had told me the difference between mourning and grieving. Back then, my world had just been rocked by my dad's death. I'd forgotten how devastated I'd been. Now, engulfed by some of those same feelings, I sat on the shore with a horse that I would never ride again.

I tried to think of some of Mr. Lambrusco's consoling words, but I couldn't focus on anything helpful. I was miserable in my wet clothes and felt a deep chill as the clouds grew heavier.

I fought to keep from drowning in depression . . . struggling to keep above water in my thinking. Then Mr. Lambrusco's words came. "It's natural to mourn the loss of a loved one, but grieving, if not checked, can tear you up inside."

By now I was shivering. Alone, with no food and facing a night in the open, I sat on the log and stared at my dead horse.

Then a fierce desire welled up inside. I couldn't just leave Jasper here! I had to find a way to bury him.

Yes! I owed him that. I would bury him right here on the

bank of the mighty Columbia River, or I'd die from the effort of it.

Think! What to do next!

I needed a shovel. More than food, a fire, or even a way to get home, I wanted a shovel!

I peered over my shoulder in order to scan the section of the trail that ran along this Washington side. A passer-by might have a shovel.

Up on the trail, I spotted a man and a pack animal. Could I intercept him?

But, just then, I looked around to see two scruffy men, sitting on a log staring at me!

Both wore ragged clothes with sweat-stained cowboy hats, long hair and untrimmed beards. I didn't like the looks of them.

I fought down fear; I had nothing for them to steal.

The larger of the two got up and walked over to me.

"Well, young feller me lad, you certainly 'pear to be on hard times. I'm Jitter, and this here is my partner, Cheet."

As Jitter came near I got a whiff of an ugly odor. Ugh! What a stench! I must have made a face, because Jitter reacted by moving downwind from me.

Sitting on the log I'd brought in, he looked at me kindly. "We came down here to help."

"Do you have a shovel I could borrow?"

Jitter frowned. "Shovel! So, you thinkin' of buryin' him."

I just stared back, too depressed to answer.

"Cheet!" he yelled. "Git up to the wagon and bring the young feller that spade from in back."

Cheet stood up and stamped his foot. "What fer? So's he kin bury the hoss? We don't want that!"

Jitter gave Cheet a baleful look. "Now hush up an' jus' fetch the shovel like I asked."

I could hear Cheet muttering under his breath all the way up to the road and back. When he threw the shovel down at my feet, I noticed that he smelled bad too.

Both Jitter and Cheet sat the log. They watched as I began the daunting task of digging a large hole in the riverbank.

To help pass the time, Jitter pulled out a clasp knife and sliced up an apple and slowly ate each slice.

Ten minutes of steady digging produced little headway with the hole. My shovel had hit a layer of clay-like material.

I plopped down exhausted and put my head between my knees.

After a minute, Jitter came over, picked up his spade and jammed it into the hard material.

"Humm, 'fraid you've hit hardpan. Even dynamite won't blow a hole in that stuff. Yer gonna hafta start over in another place."

"Start over? I can't. It'll be dark before I'd get anywhere in a new place."

Jitter gazed up at the sky. "Yeah, it would, and before then, them buzzards would be getting' pesky."

Horrified, I looked up and shuddered at two large, ugly birds circling overhead.

He'd been patient, but now Jitter got down to business. "So why don't you let me and Cheet here help you out."

"Help? How?"

"Well, young feller, you're in luck. Ya see, me and Cheet . . . we're in the compost and fertilizer business."

"Compost?" For the first time I took a close look at their wagon up on the road with its sign:

WANTED - DEAD OR WORTHLESS ANIMALS
J & C COMPOST COMPANY
I jumped to my feet. NO! NO! You can't have him to . . .

do whatever you do.

"Wal, young feller, the way a lot of folks see it, this is the best way. Our compost from cremated animals in a sawdust mulch is fine fer startin' new trees and plants of all sorts. Farmers from far and near know it helps grow good things fer 'em."

I sat down fighting back tears . . . so weary that when I tried to bring "cremated" to mind, it was like lifting a shovel of sand to the surface.

Jitter let me sort things out a while, then he added, "Ya know, we figured yer hoss wouldn't live fer long after goin' over the falls . . . not if he got bashed on the rocks below. We caught sight of him and woulda brought him in, but you beat us to em . . . clean as a whistle you did.

"He's still my horse!" I growled.

"Yes, he is. I'll not dispute that."

I wanted to go on, give Jasper a burial on the bank of the river, but I realized that it was hopeless.

"You just want me to give him to you?"

"Sometimes we buy prime animals like yours."

I took stock. I needed help to get back home. Common sense took hold. Penniless and alone, I needed money.

"How much?" I asked.

"One dollar. That's more than usual."

Survivor instinct took over. "How much for the saddle?"

"Five."

"It may be wet, but I've kept it oiled. It'll come right back . . . it's a fine piece of workmanship. I should get at least twenty for it."

Jitter glared at me. "Ya know young feller, yer not 'xactly in a position to bargain.

Seven for the hoss and saddle, total."

I saw Cheet shake his head in disagreement and sensed I'd better take the deal.

"Done. But I keep the bridle and the saddlebag."

Jitter looked over to Cheet who nodded. Then he pulled out a leather wallet and handed over a five dollar bill and two ones.

"Git ready to winch him up, Cheet, while I pull the saddle offun 'im."

I gave Jasper one more hug and gently removed the silver-linked bridle.

I turned to Jitter who already had the cinch released. "We didn't talk about the saddle blanket."

"It's part of our deal."

"All right, but I want to pull his right rear shoe . . . as a remembrance of him."

When Jitter hesitated. I jumped in. "Please, you've gotta give me that!"

"Well I 'speck a shoe for a blanket's fair enough."

"Thanks. Will you pull it for me?"

Jitter turned to Cheet who'd brought the wagon down and was about to winch poor Jasper up to the tailgate. "Bring the nail puller!"

Cheet handed over the puller. I watched Jitter expertly remove the shoe and noticed out of the corner of my eye, Cheet stoop and pick something up on his way to the wagon, but thought nothing of it.

About to drive off, Cheet glared back at me. "Ya'll pretty dang lucky, Dude. Mos' times, folks pay US to take their animals away."

As the sun set over the waters of the Columbia, I wiped a tear from the corner of my eye as my horse and the J & C Compost wagon trundled up to the road and disappeared.

twenty-six

GETTING BACK ON TRACK

A light breeze sprang up, making me even colder. Why hadn't I asked Jitter to build a fire for me before he left?

I needed to get back home. Maybe up on the road I could hitch a ride with a passerby.

But then, as in a dream, someone came toward me with such grace and smoothness I questioned my weary eyes. Was I imagining this young woman who came up and handed me a blanket?

"We were fishing when your horse went over. I am sorry. Put the blanket over you and take off your wet clothes while I build a fire to dry them."

Numb with cold and the shock of losing Jasper, I pulled the fine woolen blanket around me and did as she asked. Then I lay down on the riverbank as a fire blazed up nearby. Sleep came quickly.

I awoke to a dark sky, snug in my blanket with dry clothes and boots placed beside me. The fire had died down some, but warmth still came from it.

The girl was sitting on the other side of the fire. "My family calls me Redwing. I have brought some fish for you."

An aroma of salmon baked on a reflector board lifted my spirits.

"Thanks Redwing, I'm Casey. You're very kind."

"My mother sent the fish. My father wants you to have the blanket as a gift.

"Thank them for me."

"We are also grateful to you. We are sad at the death of your horse, but pleased that you kept the ferry from washing over the falls. It would have been much worse to see you and the ferryman killed. Then, we would have had to deal with the wreck as well . . . very bad for our fishing."

As I stared at Redwing in gratitude, she went on.

"I know the sorrow of losing someone to the falls. Last year, my uncle lost his balance on the fishing perch when he netted two salmon at once. Most men have a rope tied to their waists should they fall. My uncle did not want to be tethered. He was washed down stream and drowned."

This reminded me of my loss. Sorrow drowned out words and I just shook my head.

Redwing got up to leave. "We wish you well on your journey home." she said, and disappeared into the night.

Despite a heavy heart, I downed some freshly smoked salmon.

When the morning sun woke me up, at first I didn't know where I was. Then I re-lived the awful events of the day before when Virgil had come back into my life.

I lay in the sand with eyes closed, imagining running to Jasper. In my mind, I joyfully swung into his saddle and galloped along the river to where the Klickitat flows into the Columbia. Then we veered north up a wild and woodsy canyon. We glided swiftly through the sunlit woods, fragrant with the scent of pine and cedar where large trout splashed among the rocks.

Then reality crashed through, and I remembered Jasper aboard the barge calling to me. Calling for me to save him. I snorted in remorse as I remembered seeing him wounded, struggling to shore. Oh, my horse!

The foul smell of death that I remembered from the two compost men came back to haunt me.

I jumped up, unable to bear such thoughts, and began to run along the bank. I ran, tears streaming, until out of breath. Then, panting with hands on my knees, I tried to shake off depression.

I took a deep breath, and wiped my face with my sleeve.

"Help me deal with losing Jasper and to get back to my family." I prayed.

Still in a state of shock, and filled with dark memories of Virgil Troaz, I re-lived being violently knocked off Jasper and having him stolen from me. I'd suffered trials, tracking Virgil and fighting him hand to hand. And worse by far, after the joy of getting my Jasper back again, I'd lost him forever when that dark villain tracked me down.

I moaned, "Oh God! Help me control my hatred of Virgil."

Redwing had been heaven-sent. Even Jitter, in his way, had helped. But I had to work at getting my spirits up. If I were ever to do any good, I'd have to get over my loathing for Virgil Troaz. It would take time. I could see the image of his face before me with those evil staring eyes.

I walked back to the place where Jasper had died and carefully rolled his three diamond horseshoe in the blanket. I wrapped the fish in my bandanna.

I'd intended to loop Jason's saddlebag and bridle over my shoulder, but they were gone!

Boot tracks led up to where the wagon had been. I figured Cheet had stolen them. He must have seen me put the seven dollars inside.

What a downer! I tried to cheer up with the thought that I still had a blanket, some fish, and, thank God, my canteen . . . but again, no money.

I took a last look at the river, turned and walked up to where I'd heard a train go by in the night. With a full stomach and dry clothes on my back, I set out for home.

My riding boots were dry now, though warped and hard inside. But I felt a surge of relief that my hat, attached by a lanyard, had stayed with me through everything. Now it shaded my eyes and kept the chill breeze from my head.

I took one strong stride after another. The lump on my head didn't bother me and my bruised thigh limbered up. Walking helped divert my thoughts away from grieving.

I reached the road and hiked toward the falls. Getting back to K2 would be slow, but in early morning with the breeze at my back, I rose to the challenge.

How far to Arborville? Sixty, maybe seventy miles. How many days of hiking? Five, maybe six.

My family will be worried. If the ferryman had turned Virgil over to the sheriff, the story of his re-capture might include what happened on the ferry barge. But I couldn't count on anyone at Overton Manor having heard about it. And when the ferryman last saw me, I was swimming ashore above Celilo. I needed to send a telegram as soon as possible.

Now I returned to Celilo Falls. As I came closer, the thunder of falling water rose to a roar, and the earth trembled beneath my feet. The scene was like a photo in a geographic magazine.

I knew the season for salmon to swim upstream and spawn had begun. I was eager to get home, but still, I stopped to gaze at the amazing sight of these stalwart American Indians who were attracted here by the salmon run.

Some of the huge fish were caught as they left the water and flew through the air attempting to scale the falls. Men stood on wooden platforms in the mist and fished with nets attached to long poles.

Before moving on, I felt an added sense of history when I caught sight of a few older men who fished with spears from large rocks.

Nearby, a group of women were cleaning the salmon. I noticed one woman tending large fish filets stretched on boards. She'd placed them on end and had arranged them in circle facing an open fire.

Closer to me on the bank, was an encampment where several women prepared the morning meal. One looked up and smiled. It was Redwing. I waved my hat and moved on.

twenty-seven

DRAGONS OF THE DEEP

*U*p river, glistening in the rays of a brilliant sun, the Columbia ran wide and full.

I hiked along past the falls until the astonishing sight of a boat sailing between the riverbank and the hill on the far side brought me to a sudden stop. How could a boat sail on land?

I took off my hat and scratched my head. There must be a canal around the falls on the Oregon side that allowed river traffic to travel around the waterfall.

As I watched, a wooden hulled boat some fifty feet long, made its way out and sailed onto the river. I could read LISBONA on its broad prow. A young man stood on the pitching deck. He waved his hat and called out.

"You there! Do you look for work? We need a deck hand to help catch the beeg fish."

I was desperate. Running up, I stood at river's edge. "Yes, I'll work until I find a way to get home."

The young man waved his arms excitedly, "Sweem out, I'll peek you up!

On an impulse, I leaped in and swam across the watery gap and was hauled over the rail with a grappling hook. As I tossed my blanket up, Jasper's horseshoe thumped on the deck of the boat.

"Our third man had to quit." The young fisherman smiled broadly. "Maybee you can help us out for a few days at leest? Pulling on the lines, she's hard work, no?"

"I'm Casey Jones, I'll help for a few days."

"Ahhh, thaas ver-a good. I am Pascal."

And with introductions out of the way, the LISBONA's steam engine took charge with a roar and I noticed the other member of the crew, an older man, at the wheel astern.

Pascal called out, "My Father, thees ees Casey Jones. He has come to work for us."

The man at the wheel waved a greeting. "Haloo, Casey. I am Roi LaTrue. You will pull lines for us, eh?"

Unsure of my job aboard the LISBONA, I still called out, "Yes sir I will."

To catch their salmon, the native fishermen mostly used nets on poles. "Pulling lines" was puzzling.

"Well," I thought. "It can't be much more challenging than shoveling coal aboard the Alaska fishing boat I'd worked on, the SILVER BELLE."

On that occasion, I'd been made a member of the crew against my will. At least now I'd volunteered, though at the moment, the LISBONA was heading downstream, taking me in the wrong direction.

I watched the churning wake and noticed a strong stale fish smell mixed with the acrid odor of tar that caulked the seams of the wooden hull.

Pascal announced, "We are the LaTrue Fishing Company. Beesness has been good. Today I'll bet we weel deleever a ton of the beeg feesh to the dock at Shimran.

"A ton of salmon! That's a lot."

The captain snatched off his short brimmed hat. "Oh, ho

ho! You theenk we feesh for salmon? No! No! Not salmon! We send our lines down to the bottom . . . we catch the beeg ones, the sturgeon. We get them on the line maybee a hundred feet down and our steam engine, she wind the line and reel them up."

I stood open-mouthed. "But why do I need to pull lines?"

"Ah! The engine, she breeng the feesh up alongside, but we must sweeng them on board."

I strolled back to the helm. "I don't know anything about sturgeon." I said to the man at the wheel. "They must be good to eat."

"Ah, oui! Many people in Chicago they pay beeg price for White Sturgeon steak."

"Pascal said that business is good. How many fish do you hope to catch today?"

Mr. LaTrue scratched his black beard. "I theenk we breeng in eight, maybe more."

The captain tugged on his cap and spun the wheel. "Ay, soon we drop our hooks."

My clothes began to dry in the breeze, but I shivered until Pascal brought me a jacket with a hood.

The LISBONA rocked back and forth then found her heading. A strong current hastened us to the fishing area downstream. The breeze picked up and the sun began to dry my clothes.

I walked back to where Pascal was busily readying the fishing gear. A few miles farther down, the captain brought us around. The LISBONA headed into the current with just enough power from our engine so that we could remain motionless relative to the shore.

I watched with interest as the hooks were lowered on the long line that reached to the bottom, over a hundred feet below.

All was quiet for several minutes. Then the line gave a mighty jerk, and, with a whine, tightened on the reel.

"Oh ho!" The captain shouted. "We have a beeg one on, I theenk!"

Filled with suspense, I watched the winch roll the line on the huge reel. Heavy tugging jarred the boat. Then a gigantic white sturgeon broke water off our port bow.

"Skidoo!" I shouted. "That thing is enormous!"

"Oowee! A beeg one . . . she's maybe twelve feet." Called out Pascal as he handed me a pole with a hook and ran to get another pole with a loop on the end.

A derrick mounted to a swivel, was designed to bring the fish on board. The fish line attached to a winch was threaded through the pulley at the far end. As the winch slowly brought the splashing sturgeon in closer to the prow, Pascal smoothly dropped the loop from a pole over the fish's powerful tail and began to pull.

He called out, "Now Casey, hook the line just above the feesh and pull!"

The mighty fish swished its tail, jerking Pascal forward. He was almost pulled overboard but managed to hang on.

The captain stood used a grappling hook with one foot on the prow for several exciting minutes as the sturgeon fought the line, but the three of us wrestled the behemoth from the deep on board.

I looked in amazement at our catch flopping on the deck. It was over twelve feet long and probably weighed four hundred pounds.

Skidoo! I had no idea fish like this existed anywhere in the world.

During the afternoon, we landed one after another of the big bottom feeders. Each weighed at least three hundred pounds. Then it was time to pull into the river town of Shim-ran, on the Washington side, homeport for the LaTrue Fishing Company.

After we'd pulled alongside the dock, Pascal and I slid slippery fish onto a conveyer belt that took them into a long, steel-beamed building with corrugated metal roof and sides.

As the captain watched the last of the catch move up to be weighed in, he chuckled with satisfaction. "Eenside, thee beeg feesh are cleened and cut up. Then thee ice keep them fresh. Een jus' three days, ahh Casey, so many good people back east weel be enjoying the healthy food."

He tightened the LISBONA's moorings and turned to me. "Casey, come weeth us to our home on the heel."

"Skidoo! Yes, I need a place to stay. But first, could I please send a telegram to my uncle?"

"Ahh, m'ais Oui! We take you to the depot."

We drove in a little Ford to the train station. Mr. LaTrue waited in the car outside while a smiling Pascal agreed to pay for the message that read:

UNCLE HARRY/ VIRGIL TROAZ TOOK ME AT GUNPOINT DOWN TO THE FERRY/ SHOT FERRY-MAN/ ESCAPED HERE TO SHIMRAN/ I AM FINE/ WILL GET BACK SOON AS I CAN/ CASEY

It cheered me up to be invited to the LaTrue home over-looking the river. I had imagined a modest dwelling. Instead, as the peppy little automobile chugged up the gravel road, I was surprised to see a two-level white stucco villa built artistically into the hillside. The driveway and grounds were landscaped with Mediterranean shrubs and decorative olive trees.

I looked over my shoulder as we pulled to a stop. The view of the river and Oregon's Mt. Hood took my breath away.

As we entered the side entrance, a middle-aged woman with pretty dark hair greeted us with a warm smile.

The captain waved his arm. "My dear, I wish you to know a new member of our crew, thees ees, Mr. Casey Jones. Casey, thees ees my dear wife, Marie."

"Hello, Casey. A new crew member? Are you from Portland?"

"No, I'm from up river, near Arborville. While returning from a cattle drive, I was attacked by an outlaw but escaped from him. Fortunately for me, Captain LaTrue has offered to help me get on my feet before I head back to the ranch."

"Attacked! How dreadful. Was the bad man captured?"

"I think he was. At least the ferryman had him under control when I left."

I was shown to a bedroom with a view. I placed my belongings: Redwing's blanket, my canteen, and Jasper's three star horseshoe at the foot of the bed.

Before I relaxed in a steaming bath, I checked out the bump over my ear and the black and blue areas on my thigh . . . painful, but not serious. Marie found clean clothes for me.

Later I sat down to dinner looking forward to a nice meal with the family. What a relief to be clean, warm and dry.

At table, I met Pascal's younger sister, Angelique.

Mrs. LaTrue leaned toward me. "Casey, meet our daughter, Angie. She's a senior in high school."

Seated at the table, Angie reminded me of my pretty cousin Neva with her long, auburn hair. She turned slightly toward me.

"Hello." She said with a shy smile.

"Hello Angie. We must be about the same age, I've just graduated from Arborville High."

Angie nodded but didn't reply and kept her eyes forward.

That evening as I sat in the living room, I picked up a book, Pacific Northwest Wildlife. I read that the White Sturgeon is the largest freshwater fish in North America. They date back an estimated two hundred million years and live along the west coast from the Aleutian Islands of Alaska to central California. They basically inhabit the river basins of the Sacramento-San Joaquin, Columbia, and Fraser, with the greatest number in the Columbia. They are a slow-growing fish and may live more than a hundred years. Average mature weight is from two hundred to four hundred pounds.

In 1911, the largest white sturgeon on record was pulled from the Snake River, a tributary of the Columbia. It weighed over fifteen hundred pounds and measured twenty feet in length.

The article went on to say that the sturgeon is a bottom feeder, finding food by dragging four fleshy feelers in front of the jaw. It sucks up mud into its toothless mouth as it hunts for shellfish and insect larvae.

Its meat is highly prized as seafood and sturgeon eggs or roe, is salted, seasoned and served as caviar.

I closed the book with a deep sigh of relief. The sturgeon, a fish I'd never heard of, had now given me a way to live until I headed back home.

Still, how I did miss my horse! Mental pictures of him galloping, eyes flashing and head held high twisted my insides. I always ran up stairs two at a time. Now, I labored over every step to my room.

"Keep active!" I told myself. "Get your mind off Jasper and especially don't brood over Virgil Troaz or you'll sink into a mental funk!"

But try as I would, I just couldn't keep from wondering about how the ferryman had dealt with that monster, Troaz, after taking a bullet in the shoulder. Had he been able to control the outlaw? If not, that black-hearted villain would be free to hunt me down again.

Seized by a stab of fear, I shuddered and a chill ran through me.

I crept to the window to peek out on the dark scene below.

My heart began to pound as I scanned the yard and then
peered beyond to twinkling lights on boats and barges. I heard
nothing, nor did I see anything in the shadows. Yet, beneath
sight and hearing a sixth-sense warned me that VIRGIL
TROAZ LURKED NEARBY!

twenty-eight

T. J. IN PUSUIT

*I*n the gloom of early morning, dressed in my wool jacket, I stood in the lee of the fore-deck's cabin. A stiff breeze whipped up white-caps on the broad expanse of the Columbia.

Pascal cast off LISBONA's mooring lines and, with a swoosh and a rumble, her prow cut the choppy current as she picked up speed. I shivered as rain splattered on my face.

We approached our fishing spot for the day. We lowered the line for the catch and within minutes began to bring up the bottom feeders one at a time.

For the next five days the routine remained the same . . . up early, a hearty breakfast followed by eight hours of hard work on the deck of the LISBONA. The sixth day was Sunday, and Marie announced that breakfast would be later. I loved sleeping in until about eight. After a hot bath, I found the LaTrue family at the breakfast table.

As I helped myself to a stack of delicious looking thin pancakes, Marie LaTrue leaned over the table to me and said, "Casey, we've already been to early church service. We would have invited you to go with us, but thought you needed the rest after your ordeal with the outlaw and several days of fishing."

"Thank you Mrs. LaTrue. I did appreciate the restful morning."

At that moment, there came a sharp knock at the door. A minute later, Mrs. LaTrue brought a man into the room. Dusty from riding, he stood hat in hand, piercing eyes glaring first at Mr. LaTrue and then at me.

I jumped from my chair as I recognized Deputy T.J. Torgeson.

"My sincere apologies to you-all for this interruption," he said.

After introducing himself, he quickly went on. "I'm on the trail of a dangerous and desperate outlaw. Jones here, down Oregon way, helped bring him in once. But he's on the loose again and I've tracked him to this part of the river."

My knees buckled and I collapsed on my chair as I thought, "I knew it!"

Angie looked on fearfully as TJ continued. "The varmint's name is Virgil Troaz. Jus' last week, he had a fight aboard a ferry an' shot the ferryman in the shoulder. Looks like Troaz got loose from the ferryman and threw the unlucky cuss overboard."

I had to fight to keep from groaning out loud. It was the worst piece of news I could have heard. On an empty stomach I got so light-headed I bit my lower lip to keep large black spots before my eyes from taking over.

"And now, I'm purty sure," the deputy continued, "the murderin' polecat is tryin' to take revenge on young Jones here."

At these words, I heard Angie catch her breath as she put her hand to her mouth.

"Did you see Troaz come this way?" I asked.

"No. But almost caught up to 'im last evenin'. I'd trailed the rascal past the falls and a couple of compost men'd seen 'im headin' west at the junction where he could'a gone up and over the hill. That would'a been the smart thing fer him to do. Up in the timber he coulda set an ambush fer me and lay in wait to pick me off.

But no. He came on up thisaway. I figger he's after you, Jones. Comin' on up here to Shimran don't make no sense otherwise."

I must have looked a bit pale. I felt pale. I tried to look brave and casually poured myself a cup of coffee. As I gulped down the strong, hot liquid, Mrs. LaTrue pulled out a chair for the deputy.

"Here now officer," she said. "You must be tired and hungry. Please, take a minute to rest and have some breakfast."

"Thank ye kindly, ma'm. The man at the depot said a young man answerin' Jones' description was livin' with you folks. Now that I've found Jones, here, I can take time for a bite to eat, but I'll not rest 'til I get the drop on Troaz."

TJ was directed down the hall to wash up, and everyone talked at once, asking me about the outlaw.

By the time TJ returned to the table, I had outlined my experiences with Virgil, beginning with when he'd knocked me off Jasper and ridden off on him.

TJ poured syrup over a pile of hotcakes, forking them down in minutes. This gave me a chance to announce my decision to leave the comfortable LaTrue home.

"I can't stay here another minute." I said with more courage than I actually felt. "You all have been good to me. I must repay you by moving on."

Mr. LaTrue frowned. "Casey, you've been a good deck hand for us. We owe you, but, what can I say? Now you may be placing us een danger."

Mrs. LaTrue put her hand on my arm. "Casey, before you leave, at least finish your breakfast."

I nodded and agreed to her kindness. I'd lost my appetite, but now I was back to facing survival on the river . . . not knowing when I'd eat again. So I followed TJ's lead, and as I began to fill up on hotcakes, Angie came to my aid.

"Dad," she said. "Casey can't stay here, but maybe he could join the cutting crew at our processing shed."

Pascal agreed. "That might work." He jumped up.

"Casey, we have four Chinese cutters who cleen and slice our feesh before icing them for shipment. Maybee we could put you een with them until you are out of danger."

"Ah! A ray of hope!" I thought. Then, glancing gratefully at Angie, I got a surprise. I noticed that her right eye pulled up to the right.

While in Seattle where I'd gone to get help for my injured eye, I'd seen pictures of boys and girls with this problem in a Dr. Kraft's office there. These photos had been taken before and after surgery and had shown complete recovery with both eyes focusing together. I didn't stare at her but turned quickly back to Mr. LaTrue, who nodded his approval as Angie outlined a plan.

"Dad. Isn't Chiang, the crew boss, coming over today with the week's weight and processing records?" Angie continued excitedly.

"Yes. He weel be heer soon."

"Let's tell him that Casey needs a place to hide out from an outlaw. I'll bet he'll take Casey in."

"Casey," Mrs. LaTrue asked. "Would you agree to being on the slicing crew for a few days? We can use an extra man there and it would give the sheriff a chance to find this Virgil character."

"Yes, I would. Thank you for the offer."

I finished breakfast while the LaTrue family talked over the details of getting me into a safe place. TJ pushed his chair back with a satisfied look and sipped coffee while listening to the conversation . . . some of which was in French.

"So!" Angie said with a satisfied look. "It's settled. If Chiang agrees to our plan, Dad will secretly take him back in our car to the processing shed where he'll have a chance to explain to the others that a new cutter we've just hired will be joining them. Then, a few minutes later, Casey, you will walk down to the shed. I'll dress you in Chiang's coat with a hood, and show you how to walk like him."

I saw the logic of that. If Virgil was out there, watching this house, it would appear that only Chiang came and went on foot. Mr. LaTrue, leaving by car, would seem routine.

twenty-nine

HIDING OUT

*I*n rapid fire order, we put Angie's plan into action. I met Chiang who nodded his approval for the plan to provide a hiding place for me.

With my bundle of belongings tucked under my arm, I was soon on my way down the hill to the processing plant. Dressed in Chiang's cloak, and imitating his small steps, I felt secure in my disguise. By the time I'd walked the distance to the shed on the river, Mr. LaTrue had delivered Chiang there ahead of me.

I met the other three members of the crew; none spoke English. Chiang showed me to a bunk in a small room. After he handed me two blankets and a box of matches for the oil lamp, he left with the comment, "No slicing today. Tomorrow will show how to slice fish."

It was cold down by the river. Chiang had handed me my deck-hand jacket and I returned his cloak to him.

I went to the one small window and looked out at the expanse of water rolling by. It had begun to rain. Even in my jacket I shivered in the dank, humid room just feet above the waterline. I lit the lamp for comfort and huddled under the blankets as I considered this new place to work, eat and sleep.

The fishy smell filled the room. From the minute I'd stepped inside the large shed, the overpowering stale odor had almost gagged me. As I began to explore the big shed, from time to time I put my coat sleeve up to my nose to keep from throwing up pancakes.

From the loading ramp where the catch of the day came into the building, a long cutting table began where the conveyor belt left off. Ugh! I knew that tomorrow I'd be at that table slicing and cutting.

I closed my eyes and imagined myself riding on the train traveling from New York to Washington State. Yes, just over a year and a half ago I'd met a young man, Benny, from the Bronx on that train. He'd told me that he'd lined up a job on a Seattle fishing boat. I'd showed him a letter from another aunt and uncle of mine in Seattle mentioning work for me in their seafood business. I'd imagined that I'd be slicing fish and selling it in a Seattle fish market.

It hadn't turned out that way, but now I actually would be slicing fish, and the smell was hard to take. I might be safe here, but I struggled to fight off depression.

First, getting captured and almost killed by Virgil, losing Jasper and the money Bernie had entrusted to me, and now, winding up in this awful place.

I walked past the cutting table to another long area separated by a large rubberized flap, loose at the bottom. I noticed a stack of empty crates. I assumed that the chunks of fish were weighed, dropped into the crates, and were sent on by conveyor belt. I guessed that before each crate slipped under the flap, it was topped off with ice from an overhead shoot.

I returned to my room where a raincoat hung on the wall by the door. I rolled the stinking thing into a ball and put it under my head as I curled up on the hard bunk.

I began to feel sorry for myself.

"Think of something up-beat," I said to myself. "The La-True folks were really kind. Earlier, Captain Roi LaTrue had paid me fifteen dollars cash for my wages on the LISBONA. In parting, he'd said, "Casey, I am sorree you must leeve us. We weel steel pay you for your work down een the shed, but slicers . . . they don't make so much, eh?"

"Enough of this!" I thought as I jumped off the bunk. "I'm going to look around this place some more."

I strolled past the icing area, down to the far end of the building. I'd noticed the sound of a diesel engine. I saw it through a small window in the far wall. Housed in a building of its own, it powered a refrigeration unit and icemaker.

I peered inside the cold storage area. Frosty pipes extended past two huge troughs of chunk ice. A thermometer read below freezing.

"I'd sure hate to be trapped inside," I thought. "A person could freeze to death in there."

Case after case of fish sat on the conveyor belt ready to be loaded into rail cars.

Just then, I heard the sound of a locomotive pulling up alongside the shed. A refrigerator-boxcar rumbled to a stop; with its door just opposite our cold storage area. Suddenly two Chinese workers appeared. They opened the sliding door to the loading dock and set up the conveyor to extend inside the door of the rail car.

While one of the workers rolled case after case of iced fish onto the conveyor, the other lifted and stacked them inside the car until it was full. They took a short break while the next rail car was moved into loading position.

I'd worked for a while in a Seattle salmon cannery. The main difference here was that the sturgeon was shipped fresh. I knew that these iced carloads would soon be part of a train speeding east; first up river, then on through Spokane and over the Rocky Mountains. Swiftly spanning the straight stretches across Montana and Dakota, the delicious food from the river's deepest water would be welcomed in mid-west markets.

Above the roar of the diesel engine, I heard, "So what do you theenk of eet?"

A smiling Pascal stood beside me with Angie.

Well, hello. "Interesting how ice is used to keep the fish fresh to market."

Yes, but first, the feesh mus' be cleaned out and sliced up. "Soon you weel learn how to use these."

Pascal handed over three wooden-handled slicing knives. They were like the ones I'd seen used at the Seattle salmon cannery. The thin metal blades were kept razor sharp. Pascal explained that as one became dulled with use, I was to switch to another.

Pascal then said, "Let's go een the office where we can talk."

Angie agreed. "Yes, the smell of fish is not quite so strong there."

The three of us found comfortable chairs, and Angie made coffee and handed me two sandwiches. "Here," she said. "These should tide you over 'til breakfast."

Then she asked, "Well, Casey, do you think you'll be able to stand it here? The smell is awful and the work, worse."

"Yes, I must make a go of it, Angie. I think this Troaz character would shoot me on sight if he got the chance."

Angie's true eye focused on me. "But why does he have it in for you so?"

"Because I tracked him down. I found his hideout in Oregon and, with the help of some others, brought him into the sheriff. He also thinks I stole his horse."

"M'ais Oui . . . many reesons to want to keel you," Pascal

said, shaking his head.

I briefly described how Virgil escaped, tracked me down and had taken me prisoner. During the telling of how I'd lost my horse at Celilo, Pascal seemed too shocked to comment. Angie put her hand on mine. "Oh, Casey. How awful."

I paused for a second. I could sense that Angie was kind-hearted. She probably had suffered with an eye that always looked up. Otherwise she was attractive, with her long dark hair and pretty face. Kids would probably refer to her as "that wall-eyed girl." I must find a way to tell her of Dr. Kraft.

I finished with, "But now, thanks to you, I have a safe place to stay."

Pascal and Angie had to leave.

"We'll come back tomorrow." Angie assured me.

From time to time during the night, I awoke breathing the stale air. Once, I got up, went to the little window, and after pulling and tugging, forced a thin opening. I put my nose to it for a few breaths of fresh air before sinking back onto my bunk.

The next morning Chiang led me next door to the bunk-house where the crew ate and slept. I was given a big bowl of hot mush, a slice of bread and a large cup of steaming hot tea.

Breakfast over, I expected to be shown the slicing operation, but the crew lingered over extra cups of tea. Then I realized that first the LISBONA would have to bring in the day's catch. Of course! No fish, no slicing.

After sharpening the cutting knives at a grinding wheel, the crew began washing down the work area. Chiang gave me the job of cleaning out the fish-waste bunker just below the shed. There, amid the buzz of flies, I shoveled fish heads, tails and entrails into a large barge moored at the dock. After five minutes of shoveling, my stomach cramped. Standing in muck, breathing stench, I threw up.

Up above, all three Chinese stopped working and laughed. With eyes smarting tears of misery, I yearned for just one breath of fresh air. This had to be one of the worst moments of my life, but I refused to give up. Doggedly shoveling for half an hour, I finished by grabbing a hose to flush out remaining bits of fish blood and scales.

Aboard the Seattle fishing boat, I'd had the job of shoveling coal and, at the time, I'd thought it hard. But this was worse.

I found out from Chiang that the waste-bunker was emptied onto the barge every other day. Each time the barge was picked up by a tugboat, floated out, and dumped in the ocean. I had a one-day break before I'd be called on for more shoveling.

Meanwhile, the crew scrubbed the slicing table and all surrounding areas while chattering in Chinese.

For lunch I was offered two large pieces of buttered cornbread, more mush and a slice of fried sturgeon. In the living area, the air was mildly tolerable and I was tempted to try a bite of sturgeon but ate only cornbread and mush. Strong hot tea helped to settle my still queasy stomach.

My lunch had barely settled before the LISBONA and its crew pulled up to unload its catch.

As the first huge sturgeon slid onto the cutting line, Chiang stood beside me and slit open the entire lower end of the fish. Then, he cut off the head and tail, which dropped into the bunker. Two swipes of the knife disposed of the entrails in the same way, but careful to first lift out the valuable roe, if female.

The valuable hunk of fish that remained was carefully sliced into four or five-pound chunks, rinsed with a small hose, and sent on a conveyor belt to be iced. The day's catch, all packed in ice, would spend the night in the cold room. Later, these crates would be loaded into rail cars.

And so it went for the next three days. Each night as I lay in my bunk, I had to fight down depression as I tried not to think of Jasper. I yearned for my family back in Arborville and thought of K2's fresh alfalfa fields.

thirty

WAITING WITH A PLAN

O ne evening, under the cover of darkness, Angie visited. She fixed coffee and set a little basket of delicious French pastries on the table.

I eagerly took a big bite of a creampuff as Angie spoke up. "I wanted to come sooner, but I feared that the outlaw, Virgil, might be watching."

"Well, it's best to be careful. I'm getting along fine . . . just marking time until I can make my way back home."

"Have you thought about how you'll do that?"

"With no horse, I'll have to hike home, or maybe if I've enough money, take the train."

Angie looked sorrowful. "Sorry, Casey. There are no passenger trains that run on this side of the river."

I thought of my water-damaged boots. "Well, maybe I can hitch a ride on a wagon."

"But right now Virgil might expect you'd try that and be watching."

"I suppose you're right. For now, I'll be patient and lie low."

I paused for a minute. "Angie, have you heard anything

about TJ Torgeson?"

"My father said there was a rumor that someone had seen a man who looked like Virgil up at the logging camp. Deputy Torgeson's checking it out."

"Virgil's probably living off the hundred dollars he stole from me." I thought.

"So TJ might still be around these parts."

"Yes."

"Angie, while I've been working here, I had an idea about this sturgeon processing business."

Angie brightened up. "Let me guess. Does your idea have to do with cutting or icing?"

"No."

"Hmm. Maybe a better way to get the crates into the rail cars?"

"Not that either."

Angie smiled. "I give up. What's your idea."

I longed to mention Dr. Kraft to Angie as she looked at me so earnestly. I vowed that before I headed home, I'd open up the subject and hope she'd not be too sensitive to hear me out.

"The idea has to do with the waste material."

Angie made a face. "Oh! The heads, tails and insides smell so awful! I just don't know what you could possible do about that."

"Dry it, and sell it for fertilizer.

Angie's mouth dropped open. "Fertilizer?"

"Yes, I've heard that Oregon's Willamette Valley is farm land. Most farms can use fertilizer from time to time."

"There's the Tigh Valley area across the river too. But Casey, how in the world could fish waste be dried out?"

"Have you ever heard of the J and C Compost Company?"

"Compost? Yes, there's such a business just up river from

here. Do you think they might take our fish waste?"

"Well, I'd like to find out. I think they might mix the dried fish waste with mulch from the logging camp and produce compost for new plants."

At this point, I told of how the compost men had taken my Jasper.

Angie again took my hand in hers. "Casey, how sad that your horse ended up as compost. But what you are suggesting sounds good to me. I wonder why no one's ever thought of this before? May I talk to Pascal and my father about this idea?"

"Certainly. I want you to."

As a result of our chat, the next afternoon Pascal came to where I was cutting open a big sturgeon.

"Angie told us about your ideea to make fertilizer and compost from the feesh waste."

I continued to work but answered, "It might be worthwhile talking to Jitter at the compost operation. He seems to be in charge."

"O.K. Let the crew feenish the cutting and you come weeth me." As I moved on the splattered walkway to the forward sink to wash my hands, I had to move carefully so as not to slip down into the fish waste bunker. I smiled as I remembered the stench of the compost men. If we met with them, I'd not have to feel self-conscious about how I smelled.

As we rode to the compost company's warehouse and drying operation, I hid in the back of the wagon and pulled a tarp over me just in case Virgil was watching. When we arrived, Pascal told me to jump out quickly and enter the open end of the building.

I rushed in and looked around at a huge oven, heated by a blazing firebox. Nearby, a huge stack of tree limbs and bark seemed to be used both as fuel and for mixing with the ashes of dead animals. I assumed the pile of waste wood came from the logging camp. The strong smell I'd noticed on Jitter and Cheet filled the whole building.

Cheet was busy feeding wood into the furnace. I looked for Jitter and spotted him across the way shoveling what I assumed was compost into large burlap bags. Was Jasper's remains in there? I pushed the awful thought from my mind.

Pascal and I walked around to Jitter. His eyes opened wide when he recognized me.

"Well, young feller, I didn't 'spect to see you here. You two want to buy a bag o' compost? Folks around are starting their home gardens."

Pascal shook his head. "I am Pascal. Meester Jeeter, I theenk maybe we can do some beesnees."

Pascal nodded at me so I continued. "I'm working in a fish shed, cleaning and cutting up sturgeon. I'll come right to the point. What do you think of making fertilizer from our fish heads, tails and guts?"

Jitter's mouth dropped open. "Fish waste?"

As Jitter thought about it, he leaned on his shovel and stared at Pascal. Cheet came up and stood glaring at us.

Jitter seemed to be thinking out loud. "Fish fertilizer made from sturgeon waste, hmm."

"Well, could you do it?" I asked.

"Well son. Our oven makes high quality ash from dead flesh and bone. That could include fish parts."

Then, before Pascal or I could comment, Jitter went on.

"How much you gonna pay me to take yer fish guts off yer hands?"

I had to think fast. "We'll deliver the fish waste free of charge by barge every other day. Beyond that, the LaTrue Fishing Company would ask only ten percent of the selling price of each bag of fertilizer or compost that includes fish waste."

Jitter snorted at my offer and Cheet spoke up. "Jitter, what in the Sam Hill you doin' talking 'bout drying fish!"

Pascal seemed taken aback by this, but I went on. "We've made you a business offer in good faith. I think you two should talk it over."

Cheet bristled. "We don't need to talk it over. Now git! Both of ya!"

At that, Jitter took a step forward. "Just a minute, Cheet. Let's not be too hasty here."

Cheet glared at us while Jitter stroked his chin. "Why don't you two give us a day to mull over your offer. Come back to-morra 'bout this time."

Pascal nodded. "O.K. Tomorrow wee meet again."

On our way out, I noticed Cheet scurry into a small office. I thought of demanding my saddle bag and the money he'd stolen from me, but I couldn't prove he'd robbed me. I decided not to mention it. The possible business deal was more important.

Cheet came over and stretched out his hand to me. "Here," he said with a sneer, "We found this after we 'did' your horse."

Cheet dropped a lead bullet into my hand. I was shocked to tears as I realized what it meant.

Back on the ferry, while we'd struggled, the outlaw had wildly fired his pistol and he'd not only wounded the ferry captain, HE HAD SHOT JASPER!

Then my poor wounded horse had fallen overboard, and the rocks below Celilo Falls had finished him off.

The evil smelling Cheet seemed to enjoy watching me suffer. He stood smirking as I stared at the slug.

I turned away and blinked back tears and thought, "Jasper! Jasper! You took a bullet meant for me. Now losing you is harder than ever!"

On the way back I hid in the bottom of the wagon as before. But as I bounced around under the tarp, I thought of all the pain and suffering Virgil had brought into my life.

I furiously threw back the cover and sat up. Shaking my fist at the hillside where I thought Virgil might be watching and shoouted, "Curse you, Virgil! You killed my horse, my companion! I'm tired of hiding from you! If you can see me now, COME ON! HAVE IT OUT WITH ME!"

Back at the fishing company office, Pascal and I sat down to talk.

"I theenk that Jeeter might deel weeth us, eh?"

My heart was breaking, but I got control of my feelings and gave my best answer.

"It depends on whether or not their company has customers who will pay for fish fertilizer."

Pascal nodded. "I heer that they don't have many dead animals for their beesness. They might want a steady supply of feesh."

I secretly wondered if my Uncle Carl in Seattle, who was developing a fish fertilizer business as a spin-off from his salmon canning plant, would have any suggestions for us.

Actually, I thought Pascal and Jitter would agree to a deal. That night, about to drift into sleep, I allowed myself to imagine lush Oregon farmlands; enriched with a new product produced by the J &C Compost Co.

thirty-one

VIRGIL MAKES HIS MOVE

My unpleasant job had one advantage: I got to sleep-in until nine o'clock with plenty of time for breakfast too. Now, on this day after the visit to Jitter and Cheet, I rolled out of my bunk and began the day's routine. I walked to the door and peeked out to see any sign of Virgil.

I surveyed the riverbank. Ah, no movement.

Then, to my horror, in the undergrowth above the river, a horse and rider pulled up! A man in a long cape dismounted and furtively loped across the clearing directly at me. I hadn't the slightest doubt, it was Virgil Troaz . . . he'd taken the bait, and in a few seconds he'd be at the door.

The door was locked, but I took small comfort in that. Virgil was after me, and he'd find a way to get in.

Terrified, I raced into the empty cutting room. Virgil seemed to know the place. When he found the door locked, I saw him through the office window, hunting knife in hand, heading for the loading dock with its open area.

As I scampered down the line to my cutting station, I grabbed up a slicing knife. Too late to run, I turned to face him.

Terror welled up at the thought of fighting Virgil again. This time I wouldn't be able to ward off his knife thrusts with my cast.

I blamed myself for not staying under cover in the wagon, and prayed, "God help me," as Virgil with a shout of triumph, burst through the door and was upon me.

"Hah! Now I gotcha, boy! I'm gonna slice you up in little pieces!"

I tried to fend him off, but he ignored my outstretched knife and lunged. I dodged back as his knife flashed past my throat.

Scowling hatefully he came in low with a swiping motion and slashed through my jacket; searing my side; glancing off a rib below my heart.

I screamed and desperately threw my knife at Virgil. He ducked aside, slipping on the walkway. I reacted with a kick to his shin.

He slipped again, clutched at the rail, bounced off the walkway, and splashed into the slime below.

Half crazed with pain, I clutched my bleeding side and scurried to the loading platform while the outlaw, shouting profanity and covered with muck, climbed back up seeking vengeance.

I ran outside where, minutes before, the cutting crew had finished loading the last of the iced crates into the rail cars. Only Chiang, who was up ahead sealing the car doors, remained on the platform. His back was turned as I rushed into a rail car and hid among the crates.

Seconds later Chiang rammed the heavy door shut, rotated the bar and fastened it with a metal seal, locking me in.

I heard Chiang let out a yell of surprise followed by the sound of running feet. I guessed that Virgil had appeared, knife in hand.

Virgil suspected that I might be hiding inside because I heard him trying to cut the seal from the door. But just then the train gave a lurch and began to move. If Virgil had gotten in, I would have been hard pressed to defend myself. But I'd been saved. I offered up a quick prayer of thanks as the train moved out and picked up speed.

I wondered if Virgil was on the train.

I reasoned that if he'd seen me enter the car, he might have climbed the ladder at the end of the car and could be riding on top. But Chiang had sealed me in before Virgil had come out on the loading dock. I didn't sense Virgil nearby.

Once again I'd escaped from him!

Even so, I was suffering from a gash in my side, trapped in a refrigeration car heading for some far-off city. If I didn't bleed to death first, I'd surely freeze long before this train got to its destination.

God's favor seemed to be with me, but I had to do my part. I set about to help myself.

I realized with a stab of dismay, that there was a large fan at each end of the car. Geared to the axles, they whirled faster as the train picked up speed. Besides the cold from the slowly melting ice, the fans increased the chill inside. How long did I have to live in here? I'd freeze in few hours.

I had to find some way out. Maybe there was a vent above I could crawl through. But first I had to stop the flow of blood from the searing four-inch slash in my side.

Despite the cold, I slipped out of my jacket, shirt and undershirt. Once again I felt in my boot for the knife Cal had given me. I cut and ripped strips from my undershirt and wrapped them tightly around my waist before replacing my shirt and jacket. Now the bleeding had been slowed to a trickle and the bandage helped the pain some too.

Next, I tried to see any glow of light. There was a flicker

of light as the sun's rays penetrated past the blades of the fans, but I had little hope of seeing more.

Then, high up in the corner above my head I did see a gleam of light! Despite my painful side, I climbed on top of a stack of crates and found I could easily touch the glowing area with my fingers. Thank God! I felt the outline of a vent with air exhausting out of it.

What a relief. Covered with a screen, it seemed large enough for me to get through. I retrieved my knife and began to pry it loose. One side came free, but just as I began to pry on the other, the train jerked. I tumbled down to the floor between the crates, losing my knife in the process.

Now, jarred by the fall, I screamed in pain. Short of breath and writhing in my own blood, my misery lessened after a couple of minutes. At least I hadn't banged my side on the edge of a crate. I began a search for my knife.

I felt all over the floor area, stood up and searched the crates. Running my fingers over the crushed ice, my hands became so numb I had go give up.

I sat on the floor and thought of what to do. Maybe I could pry the screen loose with my fingernails. Then, as I looked up, I saw the dim outline of my knife still stuck in the edge of the screen. Oh! Happy sight! I had a chance to get out of this death trap.

The screen came loose and I found a crank that raised the top of the vent. I put my arms through and pulled myself up.

As I sat in bright sunshine my soaring spirit sang: "I'm heading home!"

thirty-two

BACK UPSTREAM

Atop the train, I lay on my stomach to lessen my resistance to the chill wind. My nose tingled with a mix of fresh air and coal smoke flowing back from the engine. And how I did welcome it.

With no hat, I pulled my jacket collar up and tried to think of a plan. If I couldn't get off this train, with my gashed side and loss of blood, I'd probably pass out, roll off and be dashed on the rocky roadway below. Could I cheat death one more time?

I clutched the walkway as the car swayed back and forth and struggled to think of a way out of this latest crisis.

Earlier, Virgil had appeared before I'd had a chance to eat breakfast. Now weak from hunger and loss of blood, I began to lose my grip as my strength ebbed away. I thought of lowering myself back into the car. But No! I would not go back into that freezing blackness!

But how long could I keep this up?

I saw Celilo Falls go by. If I'd acted quickly, I might have climbed down the ladder and dropped off. Redwing might still be there. She would have helped me.

But all that was out of the question. My side was too painful to have climbed down the rungs of a moving train. And even so, I'd have been killed jumping off at this speed.

So what could I do except pray and hold on? Every time the car lurched, my grip became weaker. I felt my numb fingers slipping. Would the next jolt break my hold? I was one jolt away from death on the rocks below.

I tried to prepare myself. Should I try to land feet first? Would that give me a chance to survive? Would I wind up a broken, bloody mass in excruciating pain, dying a pitiful death with no one to hear my screams? Oh! What an awful thought!

On the edge of despair, I let out a wail of anguish. I couldn't possibly hang on for hundreds, even thousands of miles until this train reached its destination.

But wait! I thought, "Come on, Casey, you've worked for the railroad. You know that this train, even with its perishable cargo, won't travel non-stop.

SOONER OR LATER IT WILL STOP FOR AN ON-COMING TRAIN. Yes! This train's engineer will receive orders to move off the main line onto a siding. But when? I MUST hang on until then . . . whenever it is.

I decided to move back to the vent. I inched my way back to the opening. To put feet and legs down inside, I had to let go with both hands and roll onto my back. But if the train lurched before I could get new handholds I'd be thrown off.

I tried to choose a time when we were holding steady, scooted to get my feet over the vent and, taking a breath rolled into position.

And just then the car DID give a mighty lurch and I pitched toward the edge of the car and went over.

"NO! NO! THIS IS THE END OF ME!"

My head and shoulders bobbed over.

I saw the roadbed below shooting past at sixty miles an hour. But I hung on with one hand and my heels hooked in the opening. For several seconds I dangled back and forth, clutching onto life, fearing death below. Then I grasped another handhold and hoisted myself back up.

Taking great gasps of air, I fought to keep from passing out.

I thought, "Move, Casey, MOVE! Move to a safe position before the next sudden bump."

I got feet and lower legs back into the vent and leg muscles helped to keep me from rolling off. On my back, my suffering continued, but now maybe I could stick it out.

I held on for several long minutes, then, at last we began to slow. I rared up, catching sight of a double track. A SIDING! In minutes we pulled onto it and came to a full stop. Here was my chance to get off.

But as I pulled my legs up, I discovered they were numb . . . not only from cold, but from being in a cramped position. I needed get to the ladder and climb down, but I couldn't move my legs.

While I sat desperately trying to rub the circulation back, I looked up to see the on-coming train approaching. In minutes it would move on by. Then my train would move back out on the main line. I needed help.

I knew that someone had to work the switch as we moved back onto the main line. But the train blocked my view and I couldn't see anyone below.

Leg problems or not, I had to make my move. I slithered to the ladder and pushed myself onto it, feet first. I felt my boots on the rung and used arm strength to lower myself, both feet at a time, to each rung. When I got low enough to the ground to jump, I let go and hit the ground with sharp pain in my side.

For a few seconds I passed out. As I came to, I heard two short toots from the engine and, with a shudder, the car above me began to move. To my horror I realized that MY FEET WERE ON THE RAIL ! I jerked them back and rolled down the roadbed.

I lay panting and holding my throbbing side as the train pulled away. I'd survived.

Oh how good the sun felt! Now I had the luxury of taking things at a less frantic pace, and I rested.

It was late afternoon when I sat up and looked around. I had no desire to spend the night here.

Then I saw the ferry landing. Of course! Train sidings were sometimes placed at junctions. The ferry brought traffic over from Oregon.

I stumbled down the ramp and fell on the dock, fighting to stay conscious. Before I blacked out, I saw the outline of the ferry as it pulled in.

I awoke on a cot in a small cabin. It was dark outside.

The ferryman, a big man with yellow hair and beard starred down at me. His right arm was in a sling

"Wal, Son, we meet again." He smiled with a grin that showed crooked teeth.

"You're in luck. A bit ago an animal doctor ferried across and I got him to stitch up your side."

"Thanks." I murmured, struggling to sit up as I felt my taped side. What a relief!

I put out my hand. "I'm Casey Jones."

"Howdy. I'm Odiah Whipple. I don't just operate the ferry, I own it."

Really curious now, I went on. "The Deputy Sheriff of Benton County told me you'd been thrown overboard with a bullet in your shoulder."

"That's true. While you were wrestling with that scalawag

Troaz, I got shot. I knocked him out, but later couldn't handle him. He did throw me overboard, but I managed to get to shore."

"Did Troaz steal your ferry?"

"No. He got it docked. But then it musta took him a while to find his runaway horse, and take off down stream."

I reached in my pocket and pulled out the bullet slug. "Troaz not only put a bullet in you, he shot my horse too . . . probably why he fell in the river."

"Aww, sorry about that. I heard he went over Celilo."

"Yes, I lost him."

Odiah pulled up a chair. "So you're afoot now."

"Yes, I'm on my way back to a ranch near Arborville."

"Well, Casey, You're welcome to stay here with me for a day or so while your side mends. I've had supper, but I'll bet you're hungry after what you've been through."

"Gosh yes."

"Well, a plate of boiled fish with spuds, 'n onions is acommin' up."

So hungry even the fish tasted good to me, I munched down every morsel. After eating, I told Odiah about my adventures downstream.

After the good meal, I felt stronger. But as I drifted off to sleep, terrifying images on top a train whirled in my head. I dreamt that I fell off and awoke in a sweat.

As I lay there, a wave of homesickness came over me. Now, with a gash in my side I knew it would be weeks before I'd be back to normal. Far from home, I had nothing. Once again, I was dead broke. I'd left in a hurry. The fifteen dollars pay for working on the Lisbona, my canteen, Redwing's blanket and Jasper's keepsake three-diamond horseshoe were all left behind in my room at the LaTrue's.

But I was grateful that I had Odiah to care for me. I had

to believe that soon I'd find my way home again.

thirty-three

AN UNEXPECTED REUNION

*D*awn's first glow lit the cabin's east window when I heard Odiah getting dressed for work. With early travelers in mind, he would get the tugboat's boiler fired up, then came back to the cabin for his breakfast.

I drifted off, then awoke when sunbeams filled the little cabin with cheerfulness. But when I sat up, my slashed side gave me a sharp spasm and reminded me of my brush with death. I sat on the edge of the bunk until the burning twinges died down and I could stagger to the table.

Odiah had left a stack of hotcakes for me warming on the wood stove. I eagerly ate every one, generously saturated with molasses, along with a cup of strong coffee. The best breakfast I'd had since I'd left K2 on the cattle drive really hit the spot.

Odiah's little cabin, perched above the bank of the mighty river was primitive, but comfortable. I refilled my coffee mug and gazed out on the blue expanse of water, out to Odiah and his ferry plying its way to the Oregon side. For the first time in many days, a sense of peace settled over me. Maybe I'd left trouble behind.

Yesterday's knife fight and harrowing train ride had worn

me down. I'd lost track of the days. Now I noticed spring had greened the slopes rising from the river and the hills beyond.

I considered my next move.

How to get home? I had no horse and no money. The insoles of my boots were cracked and painful to my feet. I couldn't hike in them. My injured side made it impossible to hop a freight train . . . there had to be a better way than that anyway. But how?

I found a pencil and notepad and scratched a quick note telling my folks where I was and my intentions to return soon. I left it in plain sight. I'd ask Odiah to mail it.

While pondering my problems, hoping for some kind of break, a small miracle came floating across the Columbia River right to my doorstep.

After a quick lunch, I sat on Odiah's little front porch, looking lazily out on the tranquil waters. The little ferry chugged its way across to the landing dock just below.

Suddenly my eyes focused on the ferry's deck. A woman with long red hair like Louella's sat on the seat of a wagon. Then I noticed the young man who looked like Fred.

Could it be? It would be too good to be true. Such a happy coincidence didn't happen in real life.

I thought of Mr. Lambrusco. He'd have some wise thing to say about this.

The ferry was still too far away to be sure, and a glare of light surrounded the ferry and its passengers. But then I knew for sure that Louella and Fred were on the ferry because, tied to the back of the wagon was a large chestnut horse. It was Dublin! They were bringing Dublin to me.

With a surge of energy, I jumped up and ran down the hill to the dock. I must have looked bedraggled but I didn't care. In minutes the ferry had docked and Louella looked up.

She called out, "Casey! Casey, it's really you!"

She jumped down and ran straight into my arms.

There were hugs and kisses and then I stood back speech-less.

"Casey," she stammered, "You . . . you can be so worrisome! We heard that Virgil got loose. We were afraid he'd kill you!"

Fred rolled the wagon onto the dock and called out, "Hello Casey! Hey, didn't expect to meet up with you here."

Too pleased for words, I managed to say, "Hello you two."

Then I heard Dublin's whinney and I really got choked up as the big horse strained to get loose and come to me. Fred quickly untied his reins. Soon Dublin was nuzzling my shirt with his usual affectionate, throaty nickering.

I put my arms around him and let my pent-up emotions go with a few sobs of joy. I knew I couldn't really transfer my feelings for my dead Jasper to Dublin, but hugging this good horse sure cheered me up.

The joyful reunion continued as two men with horses came on and the ferry pulled away leaving us on the dock. By the time it had returned, I'd described the events beginning with the cattle drive.

When I came to the part about the ferry nearly going over the falls and Jasper's death, I had to stop, as the sadness of that time came back to me.

Louella gently put her arms around me. She whispered in my ear, "Casey, how tragic." She stepped back with a tear in her eye. "I know you miss him. I loved Jasper too."

I continued on with a few down-river details, finishing with "and then I hopped a freight train here."

Suddenly, many things happened all at once; the ferry land-ed, and Louella cried out, "Casey, you're white as a sheet!"

I felt light-headed. As a wagon rolled off the ferry, Fred yelled, "look out!" and reached over to keep me from falling in front of the horses.

Still weak in the knees, I tried to stand on my own as Odiah yelled, "He's got a gash in his side . . . lost a lot of blood."

Hearing of my knife wound, Louella made a quick decision to get me to the Connor farm where I could heal and I get my strength back. She turned the wagon around and drove it onto the ferry. Fred guided me over to sit on the tailgate.

With the usual whoosh, the tugboat's steam engine went to work, sending us gliding across to Oregon.

I felt energy flowing back and I didn't mind that there'd be yet another delay getting back to K2. I loved the Connor family. I was in good hands and, in this, I sensed a small miracle.

Then another emergency hit.

I heard Odiah shout, "we've got trouble!" as he scrambled on the tug's catwalk. In the excitement, he'd neglected the boiler.

"Too much steam pressure, and the safety valve's stuck!"

I knew the danger of this. While aboard the fishing boat, Silver Belle, the boiler had almost blown up. It would have killed us all . . . sent us to the bottom of the Inside Passage to Alaska.

While Odiah frantically worked to free up the valve, the ferry began to head downstream.

I cried out, "Oh gosh, not again!"

I imagined us whirling in the river's mighty current to Celilo Falls, washing over and crashing on the rocks below. This time Dublin would die and the rest of us too.

While Louella and Fred stood frozen in fear, I sprang up into the wheelhouse. I spotted the control lever, moved it to reverse, spun the wheel to port, and waited for the ferry to right itself. After several seconds we came around.

A few seconds later, Odiah cried out, "got it!" as he released some excess pressure from the boiler. I handed over control of the tug to him. We'd put another crisis behind us.

I felt weak in the knees as I climbed down to the barge. Louella ran to me and called out. "Casey, you saved us!

This time I felt Louella's strong arms around me as I fell.

The next thing I knew, we were traveling on the roadway in the gorge. I was bouncing around in the back of the wagon . . . definitely not good for my sore side. Louella sat on the seat, holding the reins. I got up on one elbow and saw Fred on Dublin, riding beside the wagon, then I dropped back to a semi-conscious state.

thirty-four

DREAM OR NIGHTMARE?

My eyes fluttered open and there was Tilly, standing at my bedside.

I murmured, "Hello, Mrs. Connor."

"Well, heaven's sakes young man," she responded. "You seem to have a special knack fer gettin' into scrapes."

She looked sharply at me while stuffing another pillow under my head.

"I brought you some of ham 'n bean soup. You need to get your strength back."

I was hungry. I slurped down the soup while enjoying a whole pile of delicious cornbread heaped with blackberry jam. I smacked my lips as I drained the last drop from a tall glass of creamy milk.

Louella came to pick up the tray. She gazed down at me and with a big smile gave me a kiss on my forehead.

"Casey, you look pleased as a calf in clover. Enjoyed the soup, eh."

"You bet! Lou, it was almost worth a stab in the side to get back here again."

"Well," Louella said kindly, "You don't need an excuse to

visit here. You are welcome anytime. But," she went on, "since you needed someplace to mend, I'm glad it's here with us. Already you're getting color back in you face."

Louella didn't realize that part of that was due to my blushing. I needed to change the subject.

"Hey, where's my pants? I want to take a stroll around outside. Is the corn crop starting to spout?"

"Not so fast Mister Knife-fighter. You need another day of complete rest, orders from the head nurse. Besides, Tilly's still trying to wash the fish smell out of your clothes."

On the way out with tray in hand, Louella closed the door behind her. There was nothing for me to do but lie back, relax, and give my side a chance to heal. I wondered if T. J. Torgeson had captured Virgil Troaz. I prayed that he had.

The next week slipped by pleasantly. The daily routine included an always delicious breakfast with the Connors, Louella teaching me how to milk a cow, wandering in the fields of sprouting corn, and yes, several fishing sessions down at the creek. The milking made me feel helpful, and I began to get up for the 4:30 morning milking as well as helping with the one in the afternoon.

Fishing was peaceful and I always caught at least one or two big ones. On the first day, as Louella pulled in a large trout, she recalled our first fishing adventure.

"Casey, I'll never forget how surprised you looked as you fell in the creek," she laughingly remarked.

"Well, I'd rather remember the surprise of finding I'd not lost the fish on my line."

As we passed the time, I told of the LaTrue's fishing operation. Louella was amazed at the description of catching and bringing in sturgeon.

One morning as I peeled the bandage off my side, Louella expertly removed the stitches and the stab wound seemed healed enough for me to try riding Dublin.

Louella, and Fred stood by as I put my foot in Dublin's stirrup and mounted up. Pain forced me to pause before setting Dublin to a canter around the paddock. He was a very smooth horse to ride.

Riding brought mental pain too . . . a reminder of Jasper. I resolved to face up to it.

Shifting my weight slightly, I favored my left side from the riding motion. I could tolerate the soreness. I took several laps around and dismounted in a swirl of dust.

"Hey there, Casey!" shouted Fred with a big smile. "Yer back in the saddle again!"

"Yes. And I'll soon get back to my life at K2."

Louella's smile seemed half-hearted. "Glad you're up to riding again. I guess we'll be missing you around here." She quickly continued, "that means I'll have to go back to doing most of the milking."

Fred led Dublin into the barn and Louella and I sat on the porch swing.

"Lou," I began, "I've been here for over a week and I've wondered why you haven't mentioned riding up to that whitewater crossing."

"Whitewater crossing?"

"Yes, the Mountain Man asked us to come back on April 10th, but I was downstream on the Columbia on that date. Did you go without me?"

Louella chuckled. "Mountain Man? April 10th? Casey, your side may be healed enough to travel, but honestly! I'm beginning to doubt if you're back in your right mind. We didn't mention it, but the first two nights you were here, you woke us up with nightmare ravings."

I was shocked. "Nightmare ravings?"

"Yes. You were running a fever at the time. Your asking

about a mountain man just now may be a holdover from your delirium."

I sat stunned for a few seconds. "Are you saying that my memory of us up in the woods, when you and I found Anton Hoffman pinned under his wagon, was just a dream?"

Louella looked at me sadly and shook her head. "Casey, try to clear your head. A man pinned under a wagon? You are imagining things."

I looked at her closely. Had she gone up to Anton Hoffman's retreat in the woods on April 10th? Maybe that was it! She'd taken Fred with her. They'd met with the Mountain Man. He'd given them a reward of some kind. Now Louella wants to keep it all instead of splitting it with me!

I put my hand over my eyes. No! How could I even think such a thing! Hadn't Anton Hoffman said that Louella had a good heart? She wouldn't hold out on me.

I tried again. "Louella, because he had an injured leg, we loaned Dublin to him."

"Casey. Don't you remember? You and I rode Dublin up the trail after we'd captured Virgil Troaz. We found Jasper tethered just up the hill a ways."

"I do remember that, but after we found Virgil's stash, we came upon the Mountain Man on the way back down."

"Casey, this may help. Just as we found Jasper, Dublin bolted and got away from us. It was too late in the day to run him down. Fred and I went back up there to search for him after you left for home on Jasper. I found Dublin in good shape and brought him back here. That's all there is to it."

I couldn't continue this conversation. I muttered, "Well, you could be right."

I was so confused that I almost believed that I'd imagined the Mountain Man.

Louella went on. "Now Casey, when you are really ready

to return home, of course you'll be riding Dublin. He's your horse now."

Then Louella smiled, "And not only that, but you'll be carrying home your share of the reward money for our bringing in Virgil Troaz."

The reward! I'd forgotten about the reward.

thirty-five

WILD HORSE ENCOUNTER

*H*ow I appreciated Dublin's smooth gait as we rode for home. Because he was such a gentle horse to ride, my side didn't complain.

I came upon the Columbia River, looked down, and my spirits took flight at its shimmering beauty.

The morning before, when I'd bid good-bye to the Connors, they'd gathered around to wish me well. I looked at their smiling faces and Louella seemed to speak for them all.

As I rode out, she called to me.

"Come back for another visit, Casey. Before summer's over, ya hear!"

"Thanks . . . looking forward to it."

And I would be back. They didn't know it, but I had a burning curiosity to ride up to the whitewater crossing, go beyond, and solve the mystery of the Mountain Man.

They had insisted that I accept part of the reward money. Now I carried five hundred dollars in my saddlebag. Uneasy riding with so much cash, I stopped at a Pendleton Bank and opened an account. I kept enough cash to re-pay Uncle Harry the seventy-five dollar cattle sale payment Virgil had stolen from me, and enough more to buy some new clothes.

I sauntered into a general store. The store clerk's frown at my scruffy appearance changed to a broad smile as I showed him some cash and announced that I needed a full riding outfit.

He was delighted to help me buy pants, shirt, jacket, hat and riding boots. I also bought a new canteen and a fine camping knife. I loved the knife's foldout features: a large blade, a corkscrew, a leather punch and a can opener.

Skidoo! I felt comfortable in my new outfit. Everything fit perfectly, even my boots. I was ready for the ride to Arborville. I began to imagine what it would be like when Dublin and I strutted down the circular drive of the ranch house, past the row of poplars, and tied up out front.

I'd gotten an early start after a good night's sleep in a small hotel, so at mid-day, Odiah's ferry came into view.

Minutes later, while leading Dublin onto the ferry barge, I smiled at the coincidence of meeting up with Lou and Fred here. Life can offer up some strange happenings.

After a cheery greeting from Odiah, I finished a simple lunch and gazed across to the Washington side. On the hill above ferry dock, I saw two men watering their horses from a trough at the railroad junction.

I recognized T J and Virgil. Virgil had his arms behind him and may have been handcuffed. TJ stood guard with his hand on his holster.

Skidoo! Now I could breathe easier. Virgil was in custody again.

My heart soared with relief and joy. I'd suffered from the weight of being stalked by a cold-blooded killer, and now my sense of humor came back as I wondered just how the intrepid deputy had captured the outlaw.

"Heck," I chuckled. "TJ probably tracked him down by following Virgil's fishy smell."

By the time the ferry docked, the two horses and riders at the top of the bluff had ridden on.

I wondered. "Should I spur Dublin to a gallop and catch up with them?"

No! I decided to continue on at a regular pace . . . in part to favor my sore side, but also I was in no hurry to meet up with Virgil again.

Another few miles of pleasant riding brought us to a railroad work crew. Winter storms had washed part of the riverbank away. The workers were re-locating the track several feet further away from the river. But first, a sheer rock cliff had to be cut away by drilling and blasting.

It was an interesting project, but I felt relief after we'd passed through the work area, and up into the Horse Heaven Hills.

I turned to see the river ablaze with amber light from the setting sun and also the beauty of Oregon's most famous mountain.

"Well, Dublin, we'll have a pleasant ride. With a full moon we'll continue on as long as we can see the trail, then light a little fire. Tonight I'll snuggle down in one of the Connor's blankets."

Dublin answered with his unique nicker, a throaty half whinny, half staccato, grunt. From the first time we'd met, after I'd been knocked off Jasper, this intelligent animal seemed to understand what was going on around us.

My thoughts drifted back to when I'd first ridden him while tracking Virgil. Back then, I'd not thought much about Dublin. I'd ridden him too hard. Never again.

I breathed in the cool, fresh air and enjoyed riding along through one of the most impressive grassy plains in the world.

After a few miles, I reined Dublin to a stop.

"Hey, there, fella, what a fine horse you are." I said while patting his neck.

Dublin actually turned around and looked me in the eye, then turned back and bobbed his head. I could almost hear him think, "I know I'm a fine horse, but what can I say?" Then he seemed to actually say it with an extra long nicker.

I laughed and thought, "Dublin you really raise my spirits."

I stood up in the stirrups in an effort to see TJ and Virgil and spotted them up ahead.

An evening breeze stirred the grass into ocean-like waves. Dark clouds began to form in the west. I wondered if we might be in for a bit of rain.

For as far as I could see, spring grass extended in all directions, but I knew that we were coming to a large cross-trail, the one that the wild horses had traveled when Jasper and I had come through here on the way to buy wool from Redwing.

And just then, I saw them. A mile or so to the east, at least fifty horses trotted on that trail. They were moving on a course that would probably intersect the one we were on. What a thrill! If Dublin sensed them, he didn't let on.

It was time to stop for the night. I slipped Dublin's saddle off and tethered him to it. I'd picked a spot where I'd noticed a small clearing and the remains of a campfire.

Just before I settled in, I looked up ahead to see the light of a fire that I assumed was where TJ had decided to spend the night with his prisoner.

I used my new knife to cut some jerky and biscuit for a simple meal, then snuggled in against my saddle. A few drops of rain pattered down but amounted to nothing. I actually got a good night's sleep with Dublin looking over me.

At morning's first light, I got myself another simple meal, Dublin some water from the canteen and headed for K2.

"Hey, Dublin, you're about see your new home and meet

some new friends." I said.

But instead of responding to me, Dublin was standing tall, ears and eyes turned ahead. Suddenly, he snorted and stamped his hooves.

He'd sensed trouble.

As I mounted up I heard shouting. Then I thought I recognized the deputy's voice.

Was Virgil Troaz trying to pull off still another escape?

I rode on and fear rose up. An inner voice shouted, "TURN AROUND! GET AWAY FROM HERE!"

Still, I moved on, slowly . . . straining to see.

I dismounted and led Dublin for another fifty yards. Two shots rang out. I looked around for a place to tether Dublin. The best I could do was to wind his reins around my bed roll that I dropped to the ground. I crouched down and ran on.

I figured that in a struggle between the two men, TJ would probably win out. But what if Virgil had surprised TJ in some way?

I heard the snorting of a horse only a few feet away. I peered above the cover of tall grass and saw Virgil!

As I watched, he moved to mount up.

Suddenly the earth shook beneath my feet. Virgil had felt it too. He stopped. His horse whinnied and reared up. As he tried to settle his horse, a thunderclap of a sound rolled across the plain.

But it wasn't thunder. I recognized the sound of a blast of dynamite from the construction site.

The horse took off across the plain dragging Virgil who clung to the stirrup for several yards then let go and slammed down on his face as I heard the rumble of horses' hooves.

Sut's friend had been trampled in a stampede.

Was I to die a hellish death in these hills named Horse Heaven?

I heard a horse galloping from behind. A stray detached from the herd?

No! I whirled around to see Dublin. He'd freed himself and had come to save me!

I mounted him on the fly and then thought of Virgil.

I could see the outlaw a few yards ahead, staggering to his feet. He looked up with terror in his eyes as the wild horses bore down on him. Dublin and I were his only chance.

I couldn't let him die. I rode to him shouting, "Get on."

Virgil grabbed my arm and hoisted himself up behind me.

When he did, the pain from the stab wound he'd given me radiated like fire and I dropped the reins.

But Dublin needed no direction from me. With every sinew straining, the noble horse took off only a few feet ahead of the herd. Within seconds, he'd opened a space ahead of the horses. He veered to the left and slowed to a trot as the herd shot by.

Still engulfed in pain, I slumped over the saddle. My hat fell off. Virgil grabbed me by the hair and threw me to the ground.

Dublin stopped short.

I looked up to see Virgil with a twisted smile pull the pistol from his belt and point it at my head.

I'd missed being trampled, but now faced death from a bullet.

But no!

Virgil's shot went wild as Dublin leaped into the air and became a bucking bronco. The fine animal had taken sides. In this showdown, he had chosen me against his former master.

As Virgil grabbed the pommel, his gun flew in the air.

With a pounding heart, I watched the contest between horse and rider.

With the skill of a rodeo star, the outlaw stayed in the

saddle. Dublin bucked with every trick a horse could try. Still, Virgil hung on.

As the twisting, jumping, struggle continued, I ran over and picked up the pistol.

Then I heard, "I'll take that!"

Behind me, barely recognizable, face covered with blood and dust, stood T.J. Torgeson.

He took the gun and shot Virgil out of the saddle.

thirty-six

BENTON COUNTY JUSTICE

*V*irgil's trial began just two weeks after the in-
cidents up in the Horse Heaven Hills.

The Benton County prosecutor had me on the witness
stand.

"Mr. Jones, I understand that the defendant, Virgil Troaz
was shot while trying to escape the custody of the Deputy
Sheriff? Is that correct?

"Yes."

As the questions continued, I tried not to look at Virgil
sitting in front of me, his arm in a sling, his dark eyes filled
with hate.

From time to time I glanced over at TJ.

He had recovered from the fight with Virgil, who had left
him for dead after shooting him in the chest and shoulder. TJ's
badge had stopped the bullet meant for his heart.

The stalwart deputy gazed at me with kindness and encouragement. He sat beaming at me with his double smile.
His good will flowed across the room to me.

The trial lasted five days and resulted in Virgil Troaz being
sent to the penitentiary at Walla Walla. His sentence was life

imprisonment with no chance for early release.

The judge disposed of Virgil's ill-gotten gains that Louella and I had recovered at the hideout. The timberland was awarded to the state of Washington, the tavern to the city of Seattle to be run as a restaurant for tourists. Half of the cash was awarded to the Connor family the other half to Benton County.

Dublin had already been assigned to me, but to my utter amazement, the deed to the fishing boat, SILVER BELLE, was awarded to me as well. I learned that the Port of Seattle agreed to moor the boat without charge until I could take possession of it.

What would I do with it? Well, several ideas came all at once. My main thought was to contact Lear Bennett and work out a plan to use it for Alaskan geologic exploration.

I could imagine Dr. Bennett heading up a summer field excursion with his students. I could enroll as a student and fit in as a crewmember.

Skiddoo! What an exciting prospect!

* * * * * * * *

Very quickly I got back into the routine of K2 that I loved.

With spring planting and calving over, I took time off from my chores each day to ride out across the fields and up into the far reaches of K2's forested areas.

I loved the sight of the dark green fields of alfalfa and the sun shining on the hills. I thrilled to the dank smells of rich farm-land giving way to the cool pine-scented air of the woods.

But most of all, I enjoyed moving in rhythm with the horse beneath me as if we were one, climbing the trail up to Cal's hideaway and beyond.

It was different now. Earlier I'd been a greenhorn. But I'd packed in a lot of experience in a short time.

The boy-to-man changes had happened while dealing

with an outlaw and being nursed back to health by an Oregon farm family. I'd been a drover on a cattle drive, a deck hand grappling with huge sturgeon. I'd even had a stint at piloting a Colombia River ferry.

But the hardest part was to lose a horse I loved. Yet, I'd found comfort in another.

While I'd been away, Bernie had put Cal in charge of developing a new breed of beef cattle, so the canoe trip into the North Cascades had been postponed.

Neva was preparing to attend college, and Collette was quite taken with a new boyfriend.

During these busy times, I'd been to dinner at Overton Manor only once. At that time, all members of the Kinsman family were as friendly as ever and we enjoyed the usual music session after dinner.

Before the meal, I'd strolled out to the garden looking for Annie. With a little thrill of satisfaction, I found her on hands and knees, pulling weeds from a patch of iris.

I knew a sense of inner peace as she reached among the bright yellow and lavender blooms. She obviously took delight in tending these brilliantly colored flowers.

She turned her head, then jumped up.

"Casey! I thought I heard someone."

She ran to me and took my hand. "Come. Let's sit in the shade of that cherry tree."

"Good idea. Why, there's a hand-carved bench there."

"Do you like it?"

I knelt down and ran my hand over the back of the bench. I admired the design of an oak branch with stems and leaves.

"Yes. It's a truly beautiful work of art."

Annie dropped her eyes and stood beaming.

"Don't tell me you made this?"

"Yes. One day I found a nice piece of oak up on the hill."

Annie squeezed my hand. "But come now and sit. We have a few minutes before dinner."

I began with, "How have all of you been getting along while I was gone."

"Well, let's start with Neva. She's brimming over with excitement these days. She'll be leaving for college in a few weeks."

"I'm glad for her. I've been thinking about taking a geology cruise to Alaska for college credit."

"Oh, Casey. That could be quite an adventure. A much more pleasant one than your Alaska fishing boat experience, I'd hope."

"Yes, I met a University professor and he's encouraged me to enroll as a student and go along on a field trip he's planned."

"Have you decided to go?"

"Well, Annie, I don't know my own mind right now. I'd like to settle in here for a little while before I decide. I feel kind of wrung out from the outlaw experience. Then there's still a loose end in Oregon I must see to."

"You have seemed a little more thoughtful, like there's something on your mind . . ."

Just then, the Kinsman family car came up the driveway. The sound of its engine drowned out our conversation. It came to a jerky stop at the side entrance. Colleen with a squeal that turned into giggling, sang out in a loud voice, "Oh, Sam, will I ever get the hang of stopping this contraption without snapping our necks."

Annie and I chuckled and watched from across the garden as Colleen and a young man jumped out of the car, laughing and chattering their way up the walkway. As they reached the door, the Ford gave one, last, back-fire, like the sound of a firecracker.

This set Colleen off with another squeal of laughter and we couldn't help but chuckle as they moved on inside.

From inside we heard Colleen sing out, "Hi everybody. I'm back from my driving lesson with Sam."

From his office, I heard Uncle Harry respond with, "Well, thank God for that! Apparently no worse for the ordeal."

I turned to Annie. "I love it here at Overton Manor. I'd forgotten how to be light-hearted."

"It won't take you long to get your famous optimism back, Casey. It's one of the things we love about you."

Then, with a sparkling smile, Annie kissed me lightly on the cheek. "Come on, let's go in to Colleen. Wait 'til you to meet Sam. He's a kick in the pants."

The time talking about Neva's excitement about leaving home and watching the fun of Collette's happy arrival had lifted my spirits.

As Annie and I walked inside, I recalled how we'd first met in the garden, not far from where we had been sitting. Still in my knickers I'd just arrived from New York, and when I'd come up to her, she'd been busily thinning a row of carrots.

I decided that Annie was very content to be here. Now she had become a young woman, but she still loved working in the garden. I loved that about her.

I began to think seriously about my future. Did I want to stay on in Arborville, learning more about K2 and railroading? Did I want to go to college? With the reward money, I wouldn't need to ask Uncle Harry to pay my way.

Also, I had a small investment in the fertilizer company set up as part of my Uncle Carl's business. I could offer the Silver Belle as an excursion boat for a geology field trip.

The next morning, I got a letter off to the LaTrue family.

Dear Mr. and Mrs. LaTrue, Pascal and Angie,
Please accept my heartfelt thanks for helping me at a time

when I really needed it. I was broke, had lost almost everything but the clothes I was wearing and was running from a vicious killer. You gave me a job and welcomed me into your home.

Your kindness didn't end there. You even took the risk of placing yourselves in danger from the outlaw who was after me, by giving me refuge.

I hope that the idea of using the waste from your operation is successful and will repay in part for your kindness and hospitality.

Possibly you can keep my blanket and keepsake horseshoe for me. I think that at some future time we'll meet again and I can get them from you.

With warm and kind regards,
Casey

P.S. Angie, last year I needed special help for an injured eye. I can recommend Dr. Kraft in Seattle who helped me. While in his office, I noticed several "before and after" photos of young people who had an unfocused eye. He apparently is skilled at correcting this condition. I found the enclosed card with his phone number and address.

thirty-seven

MOUNTAIN MAN MYSTERY

At breakfast, I sat with Bernie and Stella.

"Well," I began. "Things have been pretty lively for me lately. Getting mixed up with an outlaw turned out to be a bit hectic."

Bernie took a sip of coffee. "Ya know, Casey. Stella an' I were just commentin' 'bout that. I wonder if you fully realize how lucky you are to be sittin' here enjoyin' breakfast with us right now."

"Yes, I think I do realize it. After all, it involved death for Jasper and near death for me more than once."

Stella reached across the table and took my hand. "We both want you to know how much you have come to mean to us. Why, when you were gone, things just weren't the same. I certainly know that was the case for our Lobo, here. He kinda mopes around when you're not here to romp with him in the courtyard."

I reached down to where Lobo was sitting and patted him. "Is that true, ol' fella, do you miss me?"

Lobo responded by licking my hand and thumping his tail on the floor.

"Well, thanks for the kind words, folks. I sure missed you too. There are times when I'd just like to settle in and live the rest of my life right here on the ranch. I'd love that."

Now Lobo, Stella, and Bernie sat and stared at me. I began to feel self-conscious.

Then, Bernie broke the silence. "But?" He said with a raised eyebrow.

"What do you mean 'but'? You think I'm about to take off again?"

"Well, you have seemed a bit restless lately," countered Stella with a knowing look.

"O.K. I wasn't going to mention it for a while, but I've been putting off a piece of business down in Oregon."

Stella smiled. "Business? Could it include paying a visit to a certain young lady?"

At this, I couldn't mention anything about Anton Hoffman, so I went along with them.

"I need to check in with the Connor family, and yes, it will be nice to see Louella there."

"We thought it was something like that. Sorry to see you go again, but we understand."

So now that the Wellmans had brought up my leaving, there was no point in delaying it.

I made preparations with them and Uncle Harry to be gone for a week or so. Two days later I was ready to head for Oregon. No one else knew that my true purpose was to ride up into the mountains beyond the Connor farm, traverse the whitewater crossing and attempt to find the Mountain Man. One way or another I would solve the mystery that Louella had created in my mind.

I was certain that we had actually met Anton Hoffman. How could she forget?

* * * * * * *

Once again I rode out in the dark of early morning, now on Dublin. This time the bright constellation of Orion appeared in the sky with Leo just above the hills.

An uneventful day's ride brought me to Pendleton where again I stayed in a hotel.

After another excellent breakfast, I was on my way with a lunch prepared by the cook there.

The sun was high in the sky as I pulled into the Connor ranch. I met Tilly. Everyone else, Jeb, the boys, and Louella were out in the fields.

I wasn't disappointed by this. Actually wanted to check out the mysteries up in forest the before I talked with Louella again. But I did agree to stop in on my way back for dinner with them all.

"We'll have a big platter of fried chicken." Tilly said happily. "We'll celebrate with some fresh cut asparagus and savory potatoes."

"Skidoo!" I said with enthusiasm. "I'm looking forward to that. I can hardly wait."

For the Connor's information, I let them think that I was going to ride up to Virgil's old hideout for a last look-around.

During those dreary times down river, I'd longed to get back here. And now I found this forest even more magically alive with the wonder of nature than I'd remembered it. Oh! How I did love it.

Dublin seemed extra lively as he pranced up the familiar trail.

"Yeah, Boy. I can understand how you must feel. Just don't get any ideas about staying. K2 is your home now."

At a clearing, a spring bubbled up to form a pool. We pulled up and saw a doe with her fawn drinking there.

"The perfect place to take a break, Dublin. While you crop

grass, I'll have my lunch."

I used my new camping knife to cut the sandwich and a piece of cheddar cheese.

I sat on a log in a state of near-perfect bliss. But inside I felt excitement mounting. We were only a short distance from where I'd remembered finding Anton Hoffman pinned under his little wagon. Would I find the directions to his place under a piece of limestone where he said he would leave it?

After lunch we set out at fast cantor to the place where we'd crossed the stream the first time to travel the parallel trail.

Dublin needed no urging to head up the new trail to the very spot where I'd found the Mountain Man pinned under his wagon. There, I recognized the tree where Anton Hoffman said he would leave the directions for finding his place up on the mountain.

My hand trembled as I parted the clump of fern where the pink limestone had been placed. The limestone was gone, and there were no directions.

I rode ahead, determined to travel on. I paused at the whitewater crossing, but Dublin, eager to cross, waded in and stepped from one submerged flat area to another. In seconds we traveled across the stream to the other side.

Dublin seemed excited. I noticed a spring in his step as we cantered up the trail, heading for the high woods.

After a mile or so, I could barely see any trail at all. We continued on through a clearing of short fern and scrub oak to an outcrop of rock.

Dublin snorted, I reined him in to a stop.

I looked up and caught my breath at the sight of a man sitting at the top smiling at us. Nearby, Catsala happily gazed down at us. On a cedar branch above fluttered several white doves and one flew down and perched on his shoulder.

I'd found the Mountain Man.

"Hello there, Casey. Welcome to the mountain."

"Hello, Mr. Hoffman."

He broke into a mellow laugh. "Please, Casey. Call me Anton."

I was warmly attracted to him.

I loved his kind eyes, with the little crinkles at the corners, the sound of his voice, and his long hair draped on his shoulders. His straight nose, a bit long, set off his mouth that showed white teeth above a short beard of black and gray.

Without any urging from me, Dublin moved up to him and nuzzled his chest.

The dove returned to the cedar branch and the cougar yawned, as I slipped out of the saddle and shook hands with Anton.

"How are you, Casey."

"Well, Anton, just now, I'm feeling very relieved."

"How is that?"

"Because finding you up here has solved a mystery."

Anton knew what I meant.

"You have talked to Louella and she didn't remember helping me down on the trail."

"She didn't remember you, or anything else about that day."

Again Anton laughed. "Well, young man. You have penetrated one mystery and have observed another."

"Another?"

"Yes. Do you wonder why a mountain lion sits calmly at my side? Why the birds are so tame and how is it that Dublin is so affectionate with me?"

"Because you have a way with them." I answered.

"I do. I do. But it's more than just being friendly with them. I'll explain later. But first, come with me, Casey. Bring Dublin, we'll walk over to my cabin."

For many weeks I'd tried to imagine what might lie beyond the whitewater crossing. Now, the view of Anton's place opened up before me. What I saw left me speechless.

Here, in the higher hills, clouds dropped their moisture more plentifully, trees grew larger and the undergrowth more lush. Wild flowers decorated the open spaces and a small stream of sparkling water descended down a ravine, splashing its way to the creek below.

A lush meadow came into view and I stopped, astonished at the breath-taking sight. Just below us lay several acres of cultivated fields surrounded by forest.

Overlooking the little farm stood a cottage. Made of split cedar logs, it blended in with its woodsy surroundings. The front door and window shutters were painted with the same rose and green decorations as the elk-drawn cart I'd seen earlier. How cozy it looked under its sturdy, shake roof.

Colorful flowerbeds whose blooms set off neatly trimmed evergreen shrubs, extended on both sides of the pathway to the front door.

Nearby, several plump chickens busily scratched away in front of a small hen house. Just beyond, Anton led Dublin into a covered stall, also made of cedar. Dublin walked right in and began to munch on hay from the manger.

"He feels right at home here." Anton said with a smile.

"Now Casey, you and I can sit in the shade of my front porch while we enjoy a bit of lunch."

"Skidoo! Lunch sounds great."

I wondered what Anton would rustle up in the way of food. The ride in the fresh mountain air had fanned my appetite. Also, I was burning with curiosity. Now, maybe I'd get some answers.

We sat in hand-made chairs and Anton waved his arm out to the area below.

"You seem to like this place. Over there Casey, I tend many kinds of vegetables, and a few nut and apple trees. Some of the corn I feed to the chickens. It is enough to supply my simple needs. Off in the distance you may see a few of my sheep."

Anton waited in silence as I looked at every part of his little farm. Set in this delightful high country spot, it seemed ideal for him.

"Anton, this place is a piece of paradise. I do love it. But doesn't it get awfully lonesome for you?"

"No, Casey. It might for most. But for me the solitude here is deeply satisfying. Call me a hermit if you wish. I keep busy and love the friendship with nature, especially the birds and animals."

"That's awesome." I answered.

"While you're thinking about my life up here, I'll serve lunch."

Anton brought out two large mugs of tea; a tray heaped with fried chicken, fresh lettuce and small carrots. He ducked back inside just as a rapid-fire sound caught my ear. A minute later he appeared with a kettle of fluffy popcorn.

Anton happily announced, "Ah! It turned out well. For popcorn, my little wood-burning cook-stove has to be just the right heat."

"Mmm. What a tasty lunch, Anton! I especially love this lightly salted popcorn, and the tea is truly delicious."

Anton finished and pushed his tray aside.

"Now Casey I wish to fill you in on my background. Many years ago, my young wife and I left our home in Wisconsin and set out in our covered wagon pulled by a team of oxen, to pursue a dream. We wished to travel the Oregon Trail to the Willamette Valley which is some two hundred miles further on from here."

I reached into the kettle for a few more pieces of popcorn,

while enjoying a second cup of tea.

"We'd heard that one out of ten would die on the way, but we were young, not much older than you, Casey. We joined a wagon train in Iowa, and thought it high adventure.

It was exciting to imagine our very own farm in Oregon. We'd heard that the Oregon countryside was beautiful, the air fresh, and disease almost unknown.

"We brought along canned and dried food, bedding, keepsakes, books and clothing. We knew that the journey would be almost two thousand miles on a crude, dusty roadway.

"Then, on only the second day out, I lost my dear wife. That morning, I remember her cheerful statement, 'Oh Anton, in about three months we'll begin a new life together.' At mid-day she was too ill to eat our simple meal. That evening she was dead from that terrible disease, cholera."

I held my breath as Anton went on.

"I found a large rock and made a headstone for her grave."

I sympathized with Anton. "I lost my father. To lose someone you love is so very hard. But Anton, you're here now. You must have gone on."

"Yes, but added to all the hardships of the trail, now I carried a broken heart. I missed my beautiful bride every hour of every day. Yet, my loss strengthened me. Through the drudgery of walking the fifteen miles a day in powdery dust, over hills, through river crossings and woodlands for two thousand miles, I kept the image of her face before me."

"But you stopped here in eastern Oregon?"

"Yes, I decided to live a life of solitude, pursuing truth and wisdom. I'd brought along some of my best books. I derived satisfaction from reading them. So when I left the wagon train and came up into these hills, I knew I'd found the place I wanted to be."

"Anton, do you ever get into town?"

"Yes, I go in once or twice a year when I need something such as tea or a special tool. I pay for what I need by selling some of the things I produce here."

Anton's story explained his life as a hermit. Then he began to describe his way with nature.

"Now Casey, would you like to know how I relate to the animals and growing things here?"

"Yes, I think it has to do with your view of life."

"Exactly. I understand and love living things. This affection is returned to me. An example is Catsala. I don't threaten her ways as a cougar. She does her things and I do mine. Occasionally our lives touch, and when they do, we share a bond of love. The birds sense this too. I don't feed them . . . the wild things, that is. At times, they simply like being with me."

"You say the wild things?"

"Yes, naturally I care for the sheep and the chickens. I cultivate my fruit trees and flowers. What I give to the living things here, they give back to me. I am a happy man."

I took the last sip of tea and waited for Anton to continue.

"Now, Casey, I am going to give you a gift: Peace of Mind."

"Skidoo, I like the sound of that! The fear of Virgil Troaz is heavy on my mind."

"Why is that, Casey?"

"Because once before when I'd helped put him in jail, he escaped, tracked me down, and killed my horse. When I ran from him, he found me again and came close to killing me. Now he's been sentenced to life in jail, but the threat of him is still with me."

"The gift I give you will not only dispel the fear of Virgil, but will strengthen you to face all future uncertainties. If you confront life's challenges wisely, you will be invincible."

"I feel better about Virgil already. But what about the big issues of how I'll find just the right job, choose good friends, and find the right young woman to marry sometime?"

"Because you are a good-hearted young man, even when things go wrong, such as when you lost your father, things will work out for you. I sense that you don't always rely on yourself; you ask for help."

"Yes, that's true."

"Well, Casey, that's very important."

"Anton. Thanks for the gift of peace. I feel you have the power to give it."

"I do, and I also gave Peace of Mind to Louella."

"Louella! She's been here to see you?"

"Yes. You are surprised at that?"

"Well, I really don't know what's going on. When I talked with her about coming back up here to see you, she didn't remember anything at all about meeting you on the trail or the whitewater crossing."

Anton sat chuckling for a few seconds then continued.

"The way I understand it, her brother came part way up here on April 10th. She'd told him that they were looking for Dublin who'd run off. He stayed in camp while Louella rode up and found her way beyond the whitewater crossing just as you did today. She had lunch with me just as you are right now, took Dublin from me and returned home."

"But . . . but why doesn't she remember?"

"Because I learned how to erase part of a person's memory through a type of hypnosis."

"Hypnosis? I've heard of that. But why didn't you want her to remember you?"

"Well, I really don't have anything to hide, but I do enjoy my life as it is. You and Louella are young. It would have been difficult for you to keep from letting the rather amazing story of my life up here slip out, and then I would be visited by curious people."

"I see. So you gave her the same gift, Peace of Mind."

"Yes."

"Are you going to somehow get me to forget you?"

"Yes."

"How?"

"The tea you have just enjoyed will make you sleepy. Just after you cross over the stream and get back on the main trail, you will nod off in your saddle. After a few minutes you'll wake up and think that you are returning from the Troaz hideout."

"And I'll not remember you . . . nothing of your beautiful place up here, or our visit today?"

"Casey, you will remember nothing about me."

"But Anton, I like you. I was hoping to visit you again sometime."

"Please, Casey, understand that I must protect my life here. I would like to have you visit me again, but that is unlikely."

It was a lot to accept. My head swam with the power of this great man. Respecting his wishes, I got up to go.

Just before I mounted up, I turned to him.

"Anton, Thank you for lunch and your gift. Now I'd like to give you something."

"But, you and Louella already gave me a precious gift. You came to my aid after the wagon fell on me."

"Yes, but I want you to have this handy camping knife. You may find it useful."

Anton examined the knife and its fold-out tools.

"Casey. Your generous offer is an example of a bit of wisdom. If you give me this knife, I will find it useful, but it will deprive you of its use. The truth here is: when one gives a material thing, there is a gain and a loss. But when one gives something non-material, such as a bit of truth or love, both the giver and the receiver benefit from the gift. For instance, the more people share an inspiring thought, the more valuable it becomes."

"Thanks for that bit of wisdom." I observed. "But I don't need the knife, and I give it to you in a loving way."

"You grasp the idea. I accept this fine gift, Casey, along with your goodwill for me. I'll think of you every time I use it. Thank you very much."

Anton took my hand. "Believe the word from the highest source, we will meet again in the life to come. Goodbye for now, my fine young man."

thirty-eight

MY GOOD FORTUNE

*A*gain, the sun sparkled on the river as Dublin propelled us down the trail to Odiah's ferry. My side had healed, and my heart was singing. Soon we'd be back in Washington, heading up the trail for home.

I was satisfied with my quick trip to the Connor farm. My journey up to Virgil Troaz's hideout had been uneventful. I don't even know why I had felt that I needed to go there. As near as I could figure out, I'd used the ride up there as an excuse to visit Louella.

Anyway, the best part of the visit had been the outstanding celebration dinner at the Connor farm. Tilly and Louella had out done themselves.

There'd been the usual fried chicken, and also four roasted trout with lemon-dill sauce, a huge bowl of fresh asparagus, whipped potatoes and fresh green salad. I ate with special satisfaction some delicious cornbread. To top things off, we were served homemade ice cream, strawberries and angel-food cake for dessert. What a happy feast!

Afterwards, Jed had leaned back in his chair and raised his coffee mug to me.

"Casey, since we've known you, the Connor farm has prospered. Our good fortune is due in part to the Troaz reward money, but I gotta say, that steam-powered corn grinder has made a mighty fine boost to our makin' a go of it here."

"My time here has been big on good things for me too . . . especially getting to know all of you. It may even have been worth getting knocked off my horse." I said with a smile.

So when I said goodbye to the Connors I was saddened by the thought that I might not see them again. Louella seemed to sense the same thing and gave me a long hug.

"Hey, Casey," she said as she wiped a tear. "Try to stay out of trouble now, won't you?"

* * * * * * * *

All morning we just kept a steady gait until the mighty river came into view and I burst into song:

Oh, Shenandoah, I long to hear yooou,
Awaaay you roll-in' riv-eeer.
Oh, Shenendoah, I long to hear yooou.
A-way I'm bound to go,
'Cross the wide Miss-souri.

I pulled up and Dublin and I looked down at the sight below.

"Hey fella, do you suppose they'll ever write a song about the wide Columbia?"

Later on, Dublin and I ambled down the riverbank to the dock. The ferry was tied up there.

I hailed Odiah. "Hi there. Got room for a horse and rider?"

"Sure thing, Casey," Odiah answered. "Business is slow right now."

As I tethered Dublin to the rail, I looked down and saw a small boat tied up alongside the dock. For a few seconds I tried to place where I'd seen it before.

Then from just behind me, I heard, "Casey Jones, if I re-member correctly."

I turned to see a smiling Lear Bennett. He continued. "Your broken arm seems to have healed nicely."

"Well, Dr. Bennett." I sputtered. "It's a nice surprise to see you here, still on the river."

"Well, Casey, I just returned. I'll spend the rest of Spring Quarter charting the geology of the gorge from here on up to Lake Chelan."

"That sounds like quite a piece of work."

"Yes, and I enjoy it."

Odiah wasn't in a hurry, so Lear Bennett and I had a chance to talk. I outlined a few facts from my Troaz adventure then asked about Dr. Bennett's fieldwork.

I could have listened for hours to his interesting stories . . . exploring the vast unmapped areas of the Pacific Northwest, but after a few minutes, a wagon appeared on the far shore and I knew the ferry'd be leaving soon.

I quickly asked, "Dr. Bennett, do you have plans to re-visit Alaska?"

"Yes. I'm putting together a proposal for this summer. Funding it is a problem because transportation up there for me and my students is expensive."

"I might be able to help with that. Because I helped bring in the outlaw who knocked me off my horse, the court has awarded me a sixty-two foot fishing boat. It's moored at a Port of Seattle dock. I'll mail a letter to you officially offering it as transportation for your Alaska field trip."

Lear Bennett was obviously excited. "Casey, you might have just the solution I've been looking for. I'll be back on campus in six weeks. I'll give you an answer soon after."

"O.K. I'll look forward to hearing from you, especially since now I've completed all my high school requirements."

"Well, if we head up there, we'll arrange for you to go along as one of my students."

"Skiddoo! I was hoping I could do that."

"Good. I'll put some details in the letter."

Lear Bennett jumped in his boat and cast off and our ferry began to steam across the river.

Meeting up with Dr. Bennett was a stroke of luck. My life's fortunes had turned around. I'd been attacked and hunted, lost my horse, been threatened and stabbed, and almost shot in the head. But now, with my broken arm and gashed side good as new, I would soon be back with my friends and family.

So much for adventure! Looking back on it, I felt stronger, certainly more seasoned, enriched by knowing the Connors and the LaTrue family too. And then there was T. J. Torgeson. How I had come to respect that fearless lawman!

Never had the future seemed so enticing. I love ranch life at K2, interested in railroading, and now feel a strong urge to explore that wild country up north . . . the coastal regions of Alaska.

All this reminded me of a take-off from a poem by Keats:

"And songs unsung are sweeter still."

I patted Dublin's neck. "Yeah, Fella, when we get back, we'll ride all around K2 and you'll love it up in the woods, camping out with Cal.

"Say, that reminds me. I didn't see my new knife when we packed up this morning. How careless of me! I must have lost it up by that swift stream where we ate lunch yesterday."

Dublin wagged his head and snorted.

Bibliography

Roberts, Wilma. *Celilo Falls; Remembering Thunder.* Wasco County Historical Museum Press. 1997.

Saling, Ann. *The Great Northwest* Nature Factbook. WestWinds Press. 1999.

Ambrose, Stephen E. *Undaunted Courage, Lewis and Clark and The Opening of the West.* Touchstone Press. 1996

Hill, William E. *The Oregon Trail: Yesterday and Today.* Caxton Press. 1986

Breinigsville, PA USA
13 October 2009
225709BV00001B/9/P